The Literary Adventures of Sherlock Holmes:

A Collection of Short Sketches

Volume One

[Containing additional manuscripts found in the dispatch box
of
Dr John H. Watson
In the vault of Cox & Co., Charing Cross, London]

Edited

By

Daniel D. Victor, Ph.D.

Paperback ISBN 978-1-78705-463-9
ePub ISBN 978-1-78705-464-6
PDF ISBN 978-1-78705-465-3

MX Publishing
335 Princess Park Manor, Royal Drive,
London, N11 3GX
www.mxpublishing.com

Cover design by Brian Belanger

Also by Daniel D. Victor

The Seventh Bullet:
The Further Adventures of Sherlock Holmes

A Study in Synchronicity

The Final Page of Baker Street
(Book One in the series,
Sherlock Holmes and the American Literati)

Sherlock Holmes and the Baron of Brede Place
(Book Two in the series,
Sherlock Holmes and the American Literati)

Seventeen Minutes to Baker Street
(Book Three in the series,
Sherlock Holmes and the American Literati)

The Outrage at the Diogenes Club
(Book Four in the series,
Sherlock Holmes and the American Literati)

Sherlock Holmes and the Shadows of St Petersburg

Sherlock Holmes and the London Particular
(Book Five in the series,
Sherlock Holmes and the American Literati)

For David Marcum,
without whose encouragement
these stories would never have seen the light of day

Introduction

*A*s compiled by Arthur Conan Doyle, the original cases of Sherlock Holmes may be categorized in any number of ways. There are, for example, those that feature animals such as *The Hound of the Baskervilles*, "The Veiled Lodger," and "The Lion's Mane." Others, like "A Case of Identity" and "The Noble Bachelor," may be labeled as stories of love gone awry. Some, like "The Three Garridebs" and "The Dancing Men," feature American villains. And still others, like "The Second Stain" and "The Bruce Partington Plans," depict political subterfuge.

The eleven stories gathered together in this two-volume anthology share their own common feature. All have connections to the world of *belles lettres*, the world of literature—some to authors in particular, others to themes or stories associated with specific writers.

In both volumes, the stories appear in the chronological order of the cases they depict. Those in Volume One take place before Sherlock Holmes reappears from his presumed death at the Reichenbach Falls. The stories in the second volume proceed well into his retirement.

By way of introduction to the stories, allow me to establish their literary associations:

- "The Missing Necklace" tells of Holmes's friendship with French author, Guy de Maupassant, which led to the writing of one of the French author's most famous stories.

- "The Amateur Emigrant" pairs Holmes with Robert Louis Stevenson on the single night the writer spent in New York City.

- "The Second William Wilson" serves as a sequel to a frightening psychological tale by Edgar Allan Poe.

- "The Aspen Papers" offers Watson's account of a situation that Henry James fictionalized in his acclaimed short story, "The Aspern Papers."

- "For Want of a Sword" and "Capitol Murder" identify the role of Sherlock Holmes in two historical events—one involving the British Navy in the Mediterranean; the other, the assassination of an American governor—both occurrences originally reported by American journalist and novelist, David Graham Phillips.

- "The Smith-Mortimer Succession" that begins Volume Two illustrates a case referenced by Holmes's Boswell-like biographer, Dr John Watson, in "The Golden Pince-Nez."

- "An Adventure in Darkness" completes the story about the country of the blind first made public by author H.G. Wells.

- "An Adventure in the Mid-Day Sun" presents a case in the voice of the young American mystery writer Raymond Chandler, who in his youth served as a page-boy at 221B Baker Street.

- "The Star-Crossed Lovers," like the title, echoes the primary theme of Shakespeare's *Romeo and Juliet*.

- Finally, "A Case of Mistaken Identity" documents the meeting between Sherlock Holmes and the American novelist F. Scott Fitzgerald that took place late in the detective's life.

Let others plumb this collection for more subtle themes. From Maupassant to Fitzgerald, the authorial giants who populate the pages of both volumes are explanation enough for its title. As interesting as such literary associations may be, of course, one can never forget that these sketches depict a series of heartless criminal acts—some more gruesome than others—in the finest tradition of all the other adventures of Sherlock Holmes.

Daniel D. Victor, Ph.D.
Los Angeles, California
June 2019

Sources

"The Adventure of the Missing Necklace" originally appeared in *The MX Book of New Sherlock Holmes Stories, Part IV,* ed. David Marcum, (London: MX Publishing, 2016).

"The Adventure of the Amateur Emigrant" originally appeared in *Sherlock Holmes: Before Baker Street,* ed. Derrick Belanger (Manchester, NH: Belanger Books LLC, 2017).

"The Adventure of the Second William Wilson" originally appeared in *The MX Book of New Sherlock Holmes Stories, Part VII,* ed. David Marcum (London: MX Publishing, 2017).

"The Adventure of the Aspen Papers" originally appeared in *The MX Book of New Sherlock Holmes Stories, Part I,* ed. David Marcum (London: MX Publishing, 2015).

"For Want of a Sword" originally appeared in Holmes *Away from Home: Adventures from the Great Hiatus, Volume Two,* ed. David Marcum (Manchester, NH: Belanger Books, LLC , 2016).

"The Adventure of the Smith-Mortimer Succession" originally appeared in *The MX Book of New Sherlock Holmes Stories, Part XII* ed. David Marcum (London: MX Publishing, 2018).

"Capitol Murder" originally appeared in *The MX Book of New Sherlock Holmes Stories, Part X,* ed. David Marcum (London: MX Publishing, 2018).

"An Adventure in Darkness" originally appeared in *Sherlock Holmes: Adventures in the Realms of H.G. Wells, Volume 1,* ed. Derrick Belanger and C. Edward Davis (Manchester, NH: Belanger Books, LLC , 2017).

"An Adventure in the Mid-Day Sun" originally appeared in *Beyond Watson: A Sherlock Holmes Anthology of Stories NOT Told by Dr John*

H. Watson, ed. Derrick Belanger (Manchester, NH: Belanger Books LLC, 2016).

"The Adventure of the Star-Crossed Lovers" originally appeared in *Sherlock Holmes: Adventures Beyond the Canon, Vol. 3,* ed. Derrick Belanger (Manchester, NH: Belanger Books LLC, 2018).

"A Case of Mistaken Identity" originally appeared in *The MX Book of New Sherlock Holmes Stories, Part VI,* ed. David Marcum (London: MX Publishing, 2017).

A Note on the Text

Footnotes followed by (JHW) were supplied by Dr. John H. Watson. Footnotes followed by (DDV) were supplied by the editor.

Table of Contents

Volume One

Volume Two

The Adventure of the Missing Necklace

How would it have been if she had not lost that necklace? Who
knows? Who knows? How singular is life and how full of
changes! How small a thing will ruin or save one!
--Guy de Maupassant
"The Diamond Necklace"

I

*Throughout the decades that I chronicled the cases
of my friend and colleague, Mr Sherlock Holmes, his
criticism never wavered. Indeed, upon looking back over the
years, I can see how much his complaints had become a
continual sticking point between us.*

*Take as an example the cold February evening in '98.
Holmes and I were sitting before a blazing fire whilst a
steady rain pelted our windows.*

*"In your hands, Watson," he observed yet again, "a
story that should be edifying turns out to be merely
diverting."*

*I am afraid I rolled my eyes. I knew we had no
intention of leaving our rooms as long as the downpour
persisted. Yet my vision of a warm wool blanket and one of
Mrs Hudson's hot toddies was dashed when I realised that to
Holmes our evening together translated into another
opportunity to resurrect the same tired criticism of my*

writing that he had presented on so many previous occasions.

To be clear, I am not alluding to the annoying little side-comments he would make from time to time as in his complaint during our investigation of Wisteria Lodge that I told stories "wrong end foremost". I am, in fact, referring to the much broader kind of dissatisfaction he regurgitated with undue regularity towards my entire literary approach.

In a nutshell, Sherlock Holmes thought my emotional nature undermined his intellectual accomplishments. For instance, at the start of the case in which I met my late wife Mary, he argued that tingeing accounts of his investigations with romanticism made about as much sense as working a love story into the fifth proposition of Euclid. And on our way to the Abbey Grange just a month before our current dust-up, he had complained about my love of the histrionic.

"You slur over work of the utmost finesse and delicacy," he said to me as the Kentish train pitched and swayed, "in order to dwell upon sensational details, which may excite, but cannot possibly instruct, the reader."

On a cold winter's night like that which we were now experiencing, one might not expect terms like "edifying" and "diverting" to draw attention away from the comforts of a crackling fire. But no sooner did I hear their juxtaposition than I sensed I had to prepare anew for a fresh argument over a familiar subject. Here we go again, I thought to myself, another discussion of how the few literary embellishments I occasionally employ serve to diminish the significance of Holmes's intellectual triumphs.

None of these charges surprised me. I had always known that Holmes craved some sort of textbook to be derived from his criminal investigations. But as his promoter as well as the chronicler of his cases, I consistently sought means to engage my readers in the thrill of the hunt rather than putting them to sleep with descriptions of what were generally routine procedures.

It was not that I disagreed with Holmes's goal. Given the number of times he bested the traditional constabulary, the need for the kind of volume he desired seemed obvious. But I aimed for a grander audience than the local police force! It should surprise no one, therefore, when I confess that the more success my writing achieved in England, the more I dreamed of presenting the adventures of Sherlock Holmes to a worldwide reading public.

To this day, I maintain that in some part of Holmes's mind, he shared my point of view. Otherwise, how can one explain the contradictory stance from a man so universally identified with rationality? At the same time he criticised my accounts of his exploits, he also appeared to savour them. In his investigation of Irene Adler, did he not refer to me as his "Boswell"? At the start of our enquiry into the Baskervilles, did he not describe me as "a conductor of light"? In our search for the Bruce-Partington Plans, did he not call me his "trusted biographer"? And when the demon known as "the lion's mane" prompted him to try his own hand at composition, did he not acknowledge how much more of the tale I could have made of it?

Such obvious encouragement did little to prod me to change my style. Let someone else write the textbook Holmes desired. For that matter, let Holmes complete the task himself. In point of fact, during the train ride in Kent, he had speculated that when it came time for him to retire, he just might compile such a volume on his own.

During that cold night in Baker Street, however, Holmes could not let the matter rest. A flash of lightning punctuated my frustration, and suddenly I vowed to get to the bottom of our on-going contretemps. *I would take advantage of our enforced time together to discover the source of his lingering dissatisfaction.*

"Why is it," I asked him between rolls of thunder, "that you harbour so basic an objection to what the public find so engaging?"

"Hah, Watson," said he, filling his pipe. "You pose such a question because you've *never seen your own accomplishments twisted into something completely different—a true story made unrecognizable in a way that not even* your *romanticised writings have done. It happened early in my career, old fellow, and I've been fearful of similar distortions ever since."*

Early in his career? *Here was a history I had never heard before.*

"Who was the architect of this distortion?" I asked, eager to learn more of my friend's past.

Sherlock Holmes flashed a quick smile. "I trust I won't be the first Englishman to blame our rivals across the Channel for something I find distressing. It was the late French scrivener, Guy de Maupassant, who demonstrated to me how, in the hands of a fantasist, fundamental truth can be completely altered. The experience has served as a warning to me ever since."

"Maupassant," said I, charging my pipe with Arcadia mixture. "Do tell. I had no idea you'd ever met the fellow. Not your usual type, was he? As I recall, he'd been incarcerated as a madman before he died."

My friend shrugged. Thunder rocked the room again, and both of us took the opportunity to light our pipes. Once the silence returned, Sherlock Holmes proceeded to relate the following narrative. (Readers sympathetic to his point of view will appreciate the fact that I offer the account

16

uninterrupted by any of the appeals to emotion and drama that I have been accused of employing.)

II

In the summer of '79 [Holmes began], not long after I had taken rooms in Montague Street, I got word from my brother Mycroft that our grandmother had died. She had moved back to France following the death of her English husband, my grandfather, and the funeral was to take place in Paris. I never pretended to be close to the French wing of our family, but Mycroft—much more mobile in those days than the sedentary figure into which he has devolved—was planning to attend the interment and asked me to join him. With the chance to please my brother—not to mention the opportunity for a summer's trip to the Continent—I readily agreed.

The list of mourners was quite distinguished. My late grandmother, the sister of the artist Vernet, had frequented the highest of artistic circles—and not just those of the painters she had met through her brother. Foremost among such artists who arrived at the cemetery that day was the celebrated novelist Gustave Flaubert, whom I recognised from his balding pate and drooping moustache. By his side stood a striking young man with a thick head of wavy dark hair, a full handlebar moustache, and a subtle *mouche* just below his lower lip. As I was to learn later, the young man's mother—said to be quite close to Flaubert—had encouraged a literary relationship between the great man and her son. In fact, the young man became Flaubert's *protégé*. His name was Guy de Maupassant.

By 1879, M. Maupassant had already gained some fame as a spinner of fictional tales; but unlike so many of our modern novelists with their unbounded flights of fancy, Maupassant displayed a practical nature and cynical point of view not unlike my own—or so I thought at the time. With similar philosophies and ages—he was but four years older than I—we quickly found much to talk about once the funeral had ended.

In fact, at Maupassant's invitation, I agreed to remain in France for an extra week; and after seeing Mycroft off for England at Calais, I travelled by railway to the young man's home in Étretat, a beautiful town on the Normandy coast. Its massive chalk cliffs and magnificent blue waters put one in mind of the Seven Sisters in the South Downs. Even at so young an age—I was but twenty-five—I remember thinking that such a coastal setting would make a wonderful place to spend one's retirement.

It took very little time indeed for M. Maupassant to discover my passion for detection and to regard me as a treasure trove of possible story-lines for his writing. Now I was new at my profession in 1879 and, sensing that neither the singular facts regarding the case of the *Gloria Scott* nor the arcane details related to the Musgrave Ritual need be made known to strangers, I had few selections to offer him. Nonetheless, young Maupassant picked my brain, and I confess to enjoying his responses to my feats of deduction.

"C'est magnifique!" he was always quick to remark followed by the clap of his hands.

Fortunately, I hit upon a case, one that had taken place not long before my departure for France, that I thought would interest the writer. Not only did my investigation present a number of odd clues and a most convoluted solution; but also, as the events had occurred so recently and thus remained fresh in my mind, I was confident that I could report the facts to my new acquaintance in great detail.

"*Eh, bien*," said M. Maupassant. " Please begin."

*****

Towards the end of last November [I told him], a series of chill nights served to keep me indoors. On the evening that I discovered the initial clues in this case, however, a thaw had occurred that allowed me to resume my accustomed postprandial walks through Bloomsbury.

Cloaked in a long, warm coat, I swung open the outer door of my lodgings, passed between the pilasters framing the portal, and strode down the steps. Upon negotiating the metal gate, I immediately found myself staring up the dark and deserted pavement of Montague Street. To be fair, a few gas lamps did offer some light, and the lack of traffic was none too surprising. During daylight hours, countless visitors to the nearby British Museum filled the walkways; but in the evenings, with far fewer attractions, there was a significant drop in the number of pedestrians ambling about.

My usual route took me through Russell Square, up to the Euston Road, and sometimes as far as Regent's Park. To that end, I set out in a north-easterly direction past the familiar line of late-Georgian, four-storey row houses. With their similar *façades*—black doors positioned towards the right-hand side of two-toned brick walls (white below, dark-red above)—most of the structures looked just like the one I had exited. Black railings fronted each house; and shallow, black-railed balconies, some sporting empty flower boxes waiting for spring, looked down from above. Owing to the broad fanlights over the doors, half-circles of brightness pooled on the sidewalk in front of many an entrance.

It required but a few minutes for me to reach the confines of Russell Square. Once inside, to the accompaniment of babbling distant fountains and the snaps of breaking twigs, I crunched my way along the gravel walkways. Even in the dark, I knew there were curiosities to observe; and as was my wont, I kept a keen lookout among the holm oaks, yews and hollies for any strange flora, fauna, or bits of detritus that might stimulate my interest.

On this particular excursion, what caught my eye was a shabby grey bowler lying on the grass a few feet away. I reckoned the thing was probably just someone's lost old hat; but my enquiring mind prompted me to investigate.

The hat appeared to be a typical old-fashioned, dark-grey derby with rounded crown and abbreviated brim. Upon closer examination, however, three curiosities presented themselves. First, located on the leather band inside the crown was the distinctive imprimatur of "Lock & Co. Hatters, St. James's Street, London." Clearly, despite its scruffiness, this hat was no inexpensive head-covering. Second, there appeared on the side of the brim opposite the outer band's bow the bite marks of a small animal. Now all kinds of creatures roam the parks of London: hedgehogs, rats, badgers—as well as the more traditional dogs and cats. But due to the size, sharpness, and structure of the indentations, these marks seemed obviously feline. Fact number three created a circumstantial case as to the animal's identity: as it turned out, the bowler was resting neatly atop a small pile of what I recognised as cat droppings, waste not easily confused by the initiated with that of any of the other creatures in question.

At first glance, I had thought the singular location of the bowler to be random. Upon further reflection, however, it seemed quite evident that the hat had been intentionally dropped on exactly the spot the cat had fouled. What is more, the deep impression of the teeth-marks in the brim gave the suggestion of strong resolve. As absurd as it appeared, logic indicated that the animal had used its jaws to pick up the bowler and carry it for deposit upon its own excreta.

Much can be learned from the actions of cats, and one need not be an alienist to recognise a similarity between the behaviour of those small creatures and that of man. I myself have indicated how the cat that purrs before attacking a mouse appears no different from the human predator who hopes to distract his victim before setting upon him. With no other cases pending and a constant desire to challenge my mental skills, I concluded that there might be worthwhile insights to be derived from discovering the relationship between bowler and cat.

Though I had no idea what sort of evidence I was seeking, I attempted to scour the immediate area for clues. In truth, the nearby gas lamps did not project their light very far, and my vision was all but useless. Luckily for me, however, I literally stumbled upon an old potting shed.

Even in the darkness I could see that the small structure was decidedly run-down. Wooden sideboards hung askew; a triangle of broken glass partially filled the solitary window; shingles were missing from the roof; and the door, attached to its frame by a single remaining hinge, stood ajar. Yet in spite of this dilapidation, I realised that it was not the shed itself but rather the freshly turned earth of the surrounding flowerbed that had tripped me up. Striking a match for a better look among the shadows, I bent down on one knee to examine the soil.

Anyone familiar with cats knows that loose earth offers them the perfect toilet. Perhaps, it was the very soil before me that had originally attracted the bowler-stealing cat to the shed. Yet almost immediately I could sense that this dirt was not all that it seemed—or rather it was more than it seemed. For mixed in with the damp soil and decaying leaves was a jumble of refuse that looked and smelled strangely out of place in the gardens of Russell Square.

I scooped up a handful of the stuff in one hand and, bringing it to my nose, was instantly struck by the stench of old garbage. Next I ran my forefinger through the muck and studied the foul mixture through my glass. No wonder it stank: it was full of bits of orange peel, black pepper, coffee grounds, and pipe tobacco—a peculiar *mélange* to some, perhaps, but not to those familiar with tried-and-true methods for turning away cats.

No doubt, someone had sprinkled this mess into the soil to discourage any feral cats from nosing around the potting shed. In the process, one animal in particular had obviously taken great exception to such rudeness. Not only had the slighted cat stolen the offender's bowler from whatever perch the hat had been placed upon, but the creature had also deposited it in such a spot as to deliver a universally-understood insult—apparently, even understood by inhabitants of the animal kingdom.

I snorted loudly at the irony. Here I was, new in my career of detecting; and my first case dealing with revenge featured that of the feline variety. Yet thanks to the potting shed, one could not forget the human element; and I immediately refocused my attention on identifying a connection between the run-down structure and the owner of the hat. I pushed at the half-open door—though in spite of striking another match, I could see nothing of interest inside. Shovels and spades had long since been removed; and whilst shards and larger fragments of clay pots littered the ground, unbroken cobwebs indicated that nothing within had been recently disturbed.

I next turned my attention to the area immediately outside the shed. The darkness did not prevent me from carefully running my fingers over the boards on each wall, and eventually I came across a slat near the ground whose corner lacked connection to the joist behind it. Needing no further invitation, I slid the wood upward and discovered a moderate-sized hollow between the boards.

It took but a moment to insert my hand, encounter the knobby folds of a burlap sack, and extract it from its nesting place. Inside the bag, I found a small collection of gold jewellery—bracelets, tiepins, rings, and such. But the *pièce de résistance* appeared to be a fine-looking necklace whose fourteen identical gems mirrored the flame of my match.

And yet the reflections failed to sparkle as they should have in the facets of true diamonds. When I found that the gems would not make a scratch in the fragment of glass in the shed's window, I was convinced. In truth, the necklace held little value.

No matter the worth of the jewellery, a cloud of suspicion darkened my mind. It certainly looked like a thief's secret horde. Else, why would it be hidden in such a manner? I had no compunction about carrying away the forgotten bowler; but though I seriously doubted it, this cache of jewels might turn out to be some poor soul's legitimate collection of wealth—a poor soul, I assumed, who had no intention of letting stray cats draw people's attention to the hiding place.

Determined to learn more, I replaced the sack and its contents where I had found them; returned to the nearest footpath; and having made the decision to defer the rest of my evening walk, exited Russell Square. On my way out of the grounds, however, I cast one final look back and could not help noticing in the darkness a pair of green, almond-shaped eyes that were faithfully tracking my departure from the garden.

*****

As soon as I reached my rooms, I picked up the copy of the *Daily Telegraph* I had left lying on my desk and searched the Agony columns for advertisements regarding Lost Property. It took less than a minute to find what I was seeking. "Lost last week near Park Lane," the announcement read, "a diamond necklace consisting of fourteen similar stones on a thin, gold chain." Mentioning a reward but offering no specific amount, the listing gave one James Laws as the person to contact at a street number in nearby Bedford Place.

The description in the *Telegraph* was close enough to the piece I had found to warrant further investigation. Pleased by Mr Laws's proximity, I immediately sent a message via my landlady's son to the address printed in the column.

Although the night was growing late, James Laws sent word via the same messenger that he could come meet with me post-haste. The loss of the necklace, he wrote, had been weighing heavily on both him and his wife. Of course, I agreed to the visit.

I was at my worktable fiddling with some malodorous chemicals when I heard the hesitant knock at the door. Upon opening it, I discovered a young man in his twenties pulling at the tip of his manicured moustache. Over his left arm hung a folded long coat. Here was someone, I surmised, that hoped his sombre, store-bought suit and matching waistcoat gave him a grander appearance than that of the clerk he admitted to being.

"Mr Holmes," said he, brushing back a shock of brown hair, "My name is James Laws. When my wife Matilda and I received your message concerning the missing necklace, we felt hope reborn."

"Pray, come in and sit down," said I, waving him into my sitting room and indicating the soft chair I reserved for clients. I apologised for the chemical smell and, occupying the desk's turning chair that I'd placed opposite him, announced the bad news.

"I must tell you, Mr Laws, that I no longer have the necklace in my possession."

A wave of disappointment washed over his face, and I marvelled that an inexpensive piece of jewellery should be the cause of so much concern.

"But," I went on, "depending on your answers to my questions, I do know how to get it."

The look of hope returned. "Ask me whatever you want, Mr Holmes. Recovering the necklace is all that matters."

"I trust you won't mind, then, if I ask you to describe the piece."

In response, he reached into his jacket and produced a pencil sketch.

"Matilda drew this," said he. "She has a much better recollection of such things than I."

Before me lay a perfect likeness of the necklace with its fourteen jewels that I'd discovered in the potting shed.

"It looks to be the same article I've seen, Mr Laws."

At these words, he allowed himself a smile.

"Yet I must tell you," I went on, "that to my untrained eye, the stones do not appear to be diamonds. Have you had the necklace appraised?"

"No," said he, looking downward. "We never had the chance." Suddenly, he glanced up, his dark eyes flashing. "You mean that it doesn't have much value then?"

"I shouldn't think so. But since a theft may still have been committed, I trust that you can describe how the necklace came to be lost."

"Of course," said he, strangely energised by my low evaluation of the piece. "Last night, Matilda and I were honoured to attend a social gathering in Park Lane—a ball, actually—at the home of Mr George Rimpon, the Minister for the Committee of the Privy Council of Education. I'm employed by the Committee as a clerk, you see—though I have much loftier goals, I do admit—and my poor wife has been longing to go to any kind of social event. Mr Rimpon took it upon himself to celebrate all of his employees in appreciation of the good work we do. A number of cabinet ministers were also to be there, you see, so such a party was a god-send for both Matilda and me."

"For the *both* of you?"

James Laws cast his eyes downward again. "I'm rather afraid," he confessed, "that my wife equates the importance of my position with the number of social engagements it offers her. And this ball has been the only one."

"Quite so," said I, pressing my fingers together. "And the necklace?"

"After the *soirée* had ended and we returned home— it was about four in the morning, actually—Matilda was horrified to discover that the necklace had gone missing."

"'Horrified' is a strong word for the loss of a trinket."

"*You* may call it a trinket, Mr Holmes; but don't you see? *We* believed it to be worth a fortune. I know you must be wondering how unassuming people like ourselves could afford what we thought to be such a lavish piece of jewellery; but the truth is that Matilda borrowed it."

"'Borrowed', you say?"

"Yes. When I first told her about the invitation, she advised me that she couldn't attend because she had no appropriate frock. To make her happy, I reluctantly gave her the money I'd been saving for a hunting rifle. She bought a charming dress, but no sooner did she show it to me than she realised she had no jewellery to go with it. I suggested she wear flowers.

"'Flowers are always fashionable,' I suggested, but in response she simply cried."

I sympathised with the poor fellow, for I understood the temperament he was describing. I'd seen similar reactions during my short-lived career in the theatre. Like a neglected actress, his wife felt as if she was pining away; and here at last arrived the opportunity to appear on the stage, and she wanted to make the most of it. However high both of them wanted to climb, only Mr Laws had the opportunity. His wife, facing a life of drudgery at home, had none.

"Matilda rejected the invitation a second time, Mr Holmes; and I was beginning to grow frantic. I couldn't afford to give my employer a negative response. To my great relief, however, it was then that Matilda remembered Mrs Forrest, a friend with whom she'd gone to school. Mrs Forrest had married a wealthy man and now possessed a grand selection of jewellery. On some previous occasion, she'd offered Matilda the chance to wear a pair of earrings, and Matilda felt certain that her friend would loan her an appropriate piece for the upcoming ball. In fact, Mrs Forrest allowed Matilda to select a piece herself. It was my wife who chose the necklace. Little did I realise the trouble this transaction would create."

Laws rubbed his hands over his face, and shook his head once more.

"As soon as we discovered the necklace was gone, we immediately retraced our steps to Park Lane."

"Had you taken a cab from the ball?"

"Yes—after walking a bit in the cold, we found a hansom. We did contact the company—"

"But without knowing the cab's number," I interrupted, "you got nowhere."

"That's right, Mr Holmes. Believe me when I say that we searched high and low. Matilda remembered that the necklace had a secure clasp; it couldn't have simply fallen away. No, in the end, we were forced to conclude that the thing had been stolen."

"I take it that you went to the police with your suspicions."

"Indeed. But since no other guests had offered similar complaints, Inspector Goforth preferred to blame the entire matter on my careless wife."

I knew the policeman. "Goforth," said I, "a good man, but lacking imagination. Of course, he'd blame it on an innocent. What about your wife's friend, Mrs Forrest? How did she react upon hearing the news of her missing necklace?"

James Laws smiled. "My wife hasn't told her yet. Matilda wrote to her that the clasp had broken and that we were going to have it repaired before returning it."

"And what was her response to this presumptuous offer?" I wondered if Mrs Forrest sensed that too much was being made over a string of glass baubles.

"Matilda told me that her friend seemed more vexed about the clasp than the delay."

"Quite so," I said again.

I informed James Laws that I might have information that could shed new light on the matter. If he and his wife could wait but a day or so, this matter might reach a happy conclusion.

"I hope to hear from you as soon as possible, Mr Holmes. We must be certain about the value of the necklace. This afternoon Matilda went to the jeweller whose name appeared on the inside cover of the black satin box in which Mrs Forrest had kept the necklace. Matilda could only show him the drawing, of course; but assuming the stones to be real diamonds, the salesman put the price at one thousand pounds. *One thousand pounds,* Mr Holmes! The news was devastating. Matilda is a proud woman, sir; and we both are honest people who will undertake to do whatever is required to repay such a vast sum to Mrs Forrest. I need not add, of course, that raising so much money will probably take ten years; for certain, it will ruin our lives.

"I understand completely, Mr Laws." Without the necklace in hand, I dared not offer confirmation of my suspicions that the gems were false, but at the same time I hoped to convey my sympathy. "I'll do whatever I can for you and Mrs Laws to get to the bottom of this."

Following these words, we both rose to our feet and shook hands. Mr Laws, uncertain whether he should be exuberant or apprehensive, gave me a final nod, and walked out into Montague Street. It would take him just a few minutes to return to his wife with my report.

III

The next morning, I visited Inspector Goforth at Scotland Yard. A professorial figure behind round spectacles, Goforth stood tall with a baldhead and red side-whiskers. Whenever the light reflected off the lenses of his glasses, his eyes seemed to disappear; and it was difficult to imagine what he might be thinking. None the less, in previous dealings, he had showed that he was willing to pay attention to a young investigator like me for whom his colleagues usually had little time. This occasion was no different. Accompanied by his curious habit of waggling the fingers of each hand in the small pockets of his waistcoat, he listened to my description of the potting shed in Russell Square. The story of the vengeful cat and the curious bowler, however, did not interest him at all.

"We'll put a man near that shed," said he when I had concluded my story. "We'll watch the cache night and day; and when that rogue returns for his loot, we shall have him."

"With all due respect," said I, "such a plan could take days—even weeks, or longer."

"Do you have an alternative solution?"

I did, actually, but I thought better of announcing it. "Not as yet, inspector. I was merely lamenting the amount of time to be spent in Russell Square by your men. Personally, I will try another approach."

*****

With a storefront of small, square windows and dark brick, Lock's Hatters is an unassuming establishment at 6 St. James's Street. Outside, its most noticeable attraction is the round sign hanging above the door. The name and address of the shop appear in the same block-lettering as the imprint within the crowns of Lock's hats. Inside, the walls are piled high with white, oval-shaped boxes, pasteboard containers filled with the top hats and bowlers that have maintained the company's reputation for more than two centuries The business itself is directed by smartly dressed salesmen in frock coats, starched collars, and silk cravats.

A look of dismay from one of these persons greeted the well-worn bowler I had extracted from my Gladstone. The salesman producing the aforesaid look, however, became more sympathetic when, after offering my name, I confessed that I was a consulting detective in search of answers. I have found it to be true more often than not that once people discover they themselves are neither the presumed targets of an investigation nor the possible victims of any danger, they become most eager to lend their expertise to solving a puzzle. Whatever the cause, Mr Robbins—for that was the gentleman's name—proved extremely cooperative.

"How can I be of service to you?" he asked.

I told him of my history with the bowler and wondered if Lock's, being so traditional an establishment, might have some way of tracing the hat's original owner.

Mr Robbins smiled and motioned me to follow. We proceeded to the end of a long mahogany counter where he exhibited a strange looking device made of metal—a piece of machinery, in fact.

"This, Mr Holmes, is our *conformateur.*"

The machine resembled a short-top hat with a brim fashioned of dark metal and a rounded crown composed of some fifty, six-inch-tall, flexible black arms. As Mr Robbins demonstrated on my own head, when the lid of the crown was gently pushed down upon, the arms—the bottoms of which now tightly encircled my skull—activated tiny pins at their upper ends that perforated the sheet of paper Mr Robbins had placed upon the top of the device. In such a manner, a precise impression of a person's head—bumps, ridges and all—was conveyed through pinpricks on the paper.

From these perforations, an accurate block of one's head could be fashioned. And after steam had been applied to the interior band of a hat, the hat could be set down upon the newly formed block and moulded to its shape. When the hat was transferred from block to head, the resultant outcome was a perfect fit.

It was quite a clever device and put me in mind of the French savant Bertillon. He was just then developing his system of body-measurements called anthropometry; and I could not help wondering how he might employ such a machine to further his hypotheses about the contours of criminal skulls. *I,* however, needed more practical information.

"What happens to the perforated paper once the hat is purchased?" I asked, fearing the pages might be discarded.

Mr Robbins's proud answer, however, was exactly what an investigator loves to hear: "We keep them in storage. That way, should a customer desire another hat, he can avoid undergoing the tiresome fitting process a second time."

He directed me to a wooden cabinet whose shelves were stuffed with boxes of those perforated pages. The files were organised by surname; but, of course, I did not posses that titbit related to the man I was seeking. In a quarter of an hour, however, Mr Robbins, working backwards from the old bowler I had brought in, was able to create a newly perforated sheet. All I needed to do was sort through the files to find the paper with the tiny holes that lined up with those of the head that fit the bowler.

With the hatter's permission, I proceeded to employ what the Americans call "legwork"—that is, good, old-fashioned labour—to match the pinpricks in my sheet with those in one from the boxes of files. To determine if the holes coincided, I held up to the light one perforated page after another, placing it over my unknown hat-wearer's pattern. It should not be a laborious task, I reasoned, just a tedious one. During the course of its long history, Lock's had accumulated a great many customers.

Fortunately, the matching holes belonged to a surname near the front of the alphabet—"Dimweather"—and the work took less time than I had feared. A man called Albert Dimweather, I discovered, was whom I was seeking.

I thanked Mr Robbins for his help and even promised to return some day when I could afford to purchase for myself the handsome tweed deerstalker I had seen there on display. Once outside the shop, I hailed a hansom and was soon rattling down St. James's Street on the way to Scotland Yard.

IV

"Dimweather" turned out to be a name familiar to Inspector Goforth. The man had previously been arrested on burglary charges, but recently seemed to be succeeding with temporary employment in service. The police knew where he lived—in a boarding house just off Tavistock Square near the British Museum. To no one's surprise, it was an address not far from Russell Square.

"Care to join us, Mr Holmes?" asked Goforth, his fingers dancing in the pockets of his waistcoat.

"Of course," said I and followed him out the door.

The police van drove down Montague Street on its way to gather up Dimweather; and once we arrived at the man's residence, I followed Goforth and two uniformed constables inside. The landlady gave us the directions to Dimweather's rooms.

Goforth pounded on the door. "Open up!" he commanded. "Police!"

The door was opened by a tall, thin man in formal black livery, the uniform of a footman dressed for an evening's work. His middle-parted black hair was neatly combed; his cheeks, clean-shaven. He was holding the brim of a black short-top hat, which was turned in such a way that I could discern the name of Lock's Hatters inside the crown. A number of other fashionable hats sat on little posts positioned on a cherry-wood side-table near the door. One could not help noticing that a solitary post remained empty. Confronted by the police, Dimweather stood at attention like the most disciplined of military men and allowed the cuffs to be fastened round his wrists.

Once the man was thus secured, Goforth placed a hand on his shoulder. "Albert Dimweather," the inspector proclaimed, "I am arresting you for the theft of various pieces of valuable jewellery too numerous to itemise at this time. Anything you say may be taken down in writing and used against you at your trial."

There was no slumping in Dimweather's stature as he listened to this announcement. In spite of being manacled, he managed to place his hat atop his head. Then, accompanied by the two constables, he marched stiffly out the front door and into the police van.

During his trial at the Old Bailey, Dimweather freely confessed to committing his thefts at various social gatherings including the ball in Park Lane for the Committee of the Privy Council of Education. Whilst masquerading as a footman, he was able to commandeer wallets and watches, cop a wayward necklace, and even lift a bracelet or two.

"I'd just walk in and pretend to go to work, sir," he told the bewigged barrister. "Nobody bothered me as long as I looked like I knew my way round. All I had to do was act like a footman, didn't I? I'd help ladies and gentlemen into their coats and wraps and then slip a hand into a pocket or unfasten a jewellery clasp. Nobody noticed, did they? The police never caught Albert Dimweather in the act."

Near the end of his testimony, he admitted to managing the cache, which I had uncovered.

"Better a hidey-hole in Russell Square," said he, "than some nook in my boarding house where any busybody might peek in."

Not to mention the odd cat in Russell Square, I mused.

To no one's surprise, Dimweather was pronounced guilty and sent off to prison. Once the trial had ended, the police returned to James Laws and his wife the necklace that Dimweather had taken, reporting in the process the relative worthlessness of the piece. Though Dimweather had illegally acquired some highly-priced gems, the false necklace he had stolen from Matilda Laws had obviously fooled him as much as it had originally fooled the couple. Mrs Laws did finally return the necklace to her friend, but I do not believe the lady ever learned it had served as evidence in court.

In fact, according to Matilda Laws, the only comment Mrs Forrest made about the necklace was, "You surely took your time returning it. What if I had wanted to wear it in the interim?" She never checked to see how well the alleged broken clasp had been mended—let alone if the necklace that was restored to her was the same necklace she had loaned out. In short, she treated the necklace like the cheap piece of jewellery she knew it to be.

The story of Albert Dimweather, the man who loved hats, was not the most dramatic of my cases; and yet in the manner of drawing conclusions, its unusual aspects rendered it most instructive.

V

"An intriguing tale indeed, Holmes," said I exhaling a cloud of smoke. The hearth fire danced lower though now the room was full of tobacco haze. "But you haven't told me how M. Maupassant liked it? You've neglected to wrap up the aspect of your story that seems to have bothered you the most."

Holmes flashed a quick smile.

"Oh, he listened to the story with great attentiveness. But the features that any logical mind would consider most compelling—the human-like nature of the cat, the strange elements in the garden soil, the mechanical workings of the conformateur—*these seemed to interest him not at all. In fact, M. Maupassant ignored my feats of ratiocination and, leaning forward with a most maniacal gleam in his eye, asked me a singular question: 'What if it had taken years for the innocent couple to learn the diamonds were false—long enough, at any rate, to have ruined their lives paying off the loss?'"*

I raised my brows in horror at the thought. "But, Holmes," *I reminded my friend,* "you said that you had informed James Laws and his wife early on that the jewels were glass. And you said the police confirmed the fact."

"To be sure, Watson; and mighty happy were they both as a result. *But surely you can understand that a truthful story in the hands of a fabulist like Guy de Maupassant provides a recipe for disaster. If you could only see it, the concerns I express about* your *writings are my humble attempts to prevent* you *from making the kinds of distortions that writers of his ilk do.*"

I resented being grouped with authors Holmes thought could not be trusted. But before I could say anything in my defence, he stood up, reached for a green-covered book from a nearby shelf, and handed it to me. "The Short Stories of Guy de Maupassant" *was printed in gold on the spine.*

"It took the Frenchman a few years to twist the plot into the form he desired," *observed Sherlock Holmes,* "but read the abomination called 'The Diamond Necklace'; and then talk to me about the wisdom of putting true crime stories into the hands of* fiction *writers!*"

He left the room in a huff whilst I leaned back, pipe still in hand, and opened the pages to the narrative in question. The fire crackled in the background.

The Adventure of the Amateur Emigrant

Family and friends insisted that *The Amateur Emigrant* be pruned .
. . even though that which was excised not only was every bit as
finished as the parts deemed publishable but also was integral to an
understanding of the situation as Stevenson saw it
and to the work as a whole.
--James D. Hart[*]

I

*Rare were the days that Sherlock Holmes dragged
the large tin box into the sitting room and surveyed the
contents therein. But no sooner had I returned to our rooms
one mid-December morning in '94 than I saw him in the
centre of the floor puttering through his collection of papers
and artefacts from old cases.*

*Poor fellow, I thought, he must be seeking
distraction.*

*Following the sale of my medical practise to Verner
a few months before, my position as locum at Barts had been
keeping me away from Baker Street most mornings. Even
Mrs Hudson was off preparing for the Christmas holidays.
Holmes, having recently completed the investigation into that
business at Yoxley Old Place involving Professor Coram and*

---

[*] Introduction to Robert Louis Stevenson's *From Scotland to
Silverado*, an anthology that includes *The Amateur Emigrant*,
Stevenson's storied account of his travels from Glasgow to California.
(DDV)

the Golden Pince-Nez, had nothing else to do but rummage among his things.

Of course, *I reflected*, he might also be researching the past to shed some kind of light on a new case I know nothing about.

Whatever Holmes's reason, I should confess that the sight of the box had always aroused in me a twinge of jealousy. Careful readers will recall that the contents of the receptacle in question represented a part of Holmes's detecting career in which my role was nowhere to be found. In point of fact, the items consisted of notes and memorabilia saved from Holmes's earliest cases, those investigations undertaken before he and I met in 1881. Here were his notes on the Gloria Scott, *the Musgrave Ritual, the Tarleton Murders, and that strangest of tales involving the aluminium crutch—all fascinating glimpses into the world of crime, to be sure, but all lacking any contribution or analysis from me, the scribe Holmes once had called his Boswell.*

The bulk of the material consisted of papers gathered into small stacks, each held together by red ribbon. There were numerous such bundles, yet I knew that beneath the papers lay additional treasures, specific objects Holmes had preserved from the investigations themselves—the peg of wood and attached ball of string from the Musgrave affair, for example, or the leather hand-grip from the aluminium crutch.

"A trip into the past?" I asked my colleague.

"Quite so, Watson" said Holmes. "I have always held that a periodic review of former cases helps stimulate the brain. Through such analysis, one may discover recurring patterns in the criminal mind. You may recall how my recollection of the Hindu snake charmer of Brixton

helped me predict the behaviour of the villainous Dr Grimesby Roylott and his so-called 'Speckled Band'."

I did not recall the anecdote he cited—presumably because he had never bothered to report it to me. Yet all I said was, "Certainly, Holmes, but these things here"—I made a dismissive gesture in the direction of the tin box—"represent cases from your callow youth."

"However true, old fellow, such remembrances are still ripe for the picking—though today I must confess that I'm looking for a set of papers that are more nostalgic than instructive."

I had no idea to what he was referring, but none the less I watched him continue to riffle through the bundles. In the process an unbound collection of pages caught my eye. Unlike the other papers, which were held together by the ubiquitous red ribbon, these appeared torn from a notebook. What is more, though written in a tiny, cribbed style not unlike that of Holmes himself, the lettering on these pages appeared shaky; and the spaces between lines, much wider than in the writings of my friend.

"What are those?" I asked, pointing at the notebook pages. "They're different from the rest."

Holmes's long fingers reached for the papers I had identified and lifted them out of the box.

"The very thing I was looking for," said he. "You have excellent eyes, old fellow. No doubt, it takes a writer to spot the work of a fellow scribbler. These pages were sent to me by an old acquaintance, Louis Stevenson—Robert Louis Stevenson to the world at large."

"The Scotsman who died just the past fortnight? The writer?"

"The very same. In memory of his passing, I wanted to review an unpublished chapter from an early volume of

his. Do you know, Watson, though I don't trumpet it about, I was instrumental in inspiring one of his most famous novels."

"Surely not that scandalous thriller, Dr Jekyll and Mr Hyde? *You do know that there are more than a few naïfs who believe that the monstrous Mr Hyde was real and that Sherlock Holmes played some role in ending his reign of terror."*

Holmes dismissed the notion with a wave of his hand. "No," said he, shaking his head, "my contribution was to a more swashbuckling kind of tale."

Clearly, I was about to hear a new bit of Holmesian history. In preparation, I poured us both a glass of sherry and settled into an armchair. "Do tell," I encouraged him.

Holmes sampled his drink and then began the following account: "As you are aware, Watson, a month or so after I had come up from Cambridge, I joined a troupe of actors called the Sasanoff Company. Not long thereafter, in the summer of '79, I found myself performing on the stage in New York—that is, before I ran out of money and had to return to England. Fortunately, within a matter of months I was able to re-join the Sasanoff group."

I knew of Holmes's brief acting career as well as his appearance on the New York stage. Indeed, but a few years earlier I had written that the stage had lost a fine actor when when my friend turned his mind to criminal detection.

"As it happened," Holmes continued, "Stevenson arrived in New York in the middle of August. He was on his way to San Francisco to join the American divorcée with whom he had fallen in love during a trip to France. In point of fact, he planned to begin his railway journey west the day following his arrival."

"After just one *night in New York City, Holmes?"*

"He had Cupid to propel him, old fellow. I should have thought that a romantic like yourself would admire his haste."

"But a single night, Holmes, in so vibrant a metropolis!"

"True," Sherlock Holmes nodded, "but let us not forget that the specific night in question was the occasion of our meeting. In fact, I remember the evening quite well. We were staging a pantomime of Robinson Crusoe. It had been raining heavily, and the members of the cast were wondering how many people in search of an evening's entertainment would be willing to brave the elements. A small hole in the red-velvet curtain allowed us to scrutinise the audience as they arrived.

"'Maybe half full,' I remember Nelly Ross observing as she backed away from the velvet to give me a look. 'But better than I expected for so wet a night.'"

"Nelly Ross?"

"The ingénue playing Robinson Crusoe."

"Ah."

"With her encouragement, I too peered through the aperture. The number of empty seats was indeed sufficient to catch the eye, and yet my gaze was attracted to a slight young man just then entering the rear of the hall. It was his burgundy-coloured velveteen jacket that first caught my attention—I noted it once he had removed his wet Mackintosh. But it was his cadaverous mien that sustained my curiosity.

"His pale, oval-shaped face seemed all the whiter in contrast to the frame of dark damp hair falling almost to his shoulders. The scraggly moustache and hollow eyes set widely apart added to his frail appearance. Why, even before he reached his seat, he was covering his mouth with a *free hand, and I could tell from the shaking of his body that he was fighting a paroxysm of coughing. Only when it subsided did he settle into his chair next to the nondescript man with whom he had entered.*

"The longer I stared, the greater my realisation that there was something familiar to me about the young man's bohemian aspect. Yet it was only after he had replaced a common flat hat with a gilt-embroidered Indian skullcap that I identified him. For, you see, I had observed the same man thus distinctively apparelled at Hatchards a few months before I had left England. He had coughed then as well. It was all quite remarkable. Before me in a New York theatre sat the little-known Scottish writer, Robert Louis Stevenson.

"Though I had yet to begin my detecting career, it was the man's insightful depictions of murder that originally attracted me to his work. I need not remind you, Watson, that criminal pursuits have intrigued me from the beginning; and the passages Stevenson read at Hatchards that day were taken from a tale of death he had written two years before— one of his first, actually—called 'A Lodging for the Night'. It dealt with the reactions of the infamous French poet, François Villon, to a vicious murder. Even then, Stevenson seemed fascinated with how the soul of a poet and the soul of a criminal might be embodied in a single being."

"Jekyll and Hyde," I murmured.

Holmes nodded and continued his story. "Stevenson's appearance at the theatre that evening triggered a jumble of memories—of Hatchards, of the story he had read there, and of his haunting eyes. At the same time, however, I also knew that we had a show to put on; and with the curtain about to rise, I needed to assume my role. I was portraying a villainous pirate—a one-legged sea cook, no less—and I had to take my spot before the curtain rose.

"Happily, in spite of the incessant rain and an only partially-filled house, we put on a rousing performance that night; and to show his appreciation, Stevenson requested permission to come back-stage to congratulate the entire company. He greeted us all with equanimity, certainly having no cause to single me out in any way. No, Watson, as you might well imagine, it required a singular crime to bring the two of us together."

I am afraid I knit my brows at this last proclamation. "I can understand not hearing of such an occurrence from you, Holmes," said I, "but Stevenson was a prolific chronicler of his journeys. As I recall, he produced at least two works, Travels with a Donkey in the Cévennes and An Inland Voyage, that report his adventures on the continent before he ever wrote about his trip to America. He loved the dramatic anecdote, and yet I have never seen in print any account by the man of some crime that had been committed against him in New York."

"Quite so," said Holmes with a quick smile. He then finished his sherry and, setting down the glass, picked up the papers he had withdrawn from the tin box.

"News of our meeting," said he, '"never appeared in the published reports of Stevenson's travels in America. In the letter he wrote me that accompanied these pages, he explained that he had sent the account home for publication. In order to maintain a positive image of the writer, however, his friends and publishers chose to omit any stories they found objectionable or controversial. Apparently, Stevenson's depiction of himself as a target of a criminal in New York City stood no chance of being published."

At this point, Holmes handed me the unbound pages.

"Enough of my blather," said he. "Why not read it for yourself."

It was with great excitement that I took up the bundle. Scrawled across the top sheet in Holmes's penmanship were the words, "Excised from the chapter 'New York' in The Amateur Emigrant *by Robert Louis Stevenson (translations from the Latin rendered by S. Holmes)". My friend filled his pipe in preparation for an uninterrupted smoke; I leaned back in my armchair in anticipation of learning about the night in question from Stevenson himself.*

II

I have already mentioned my debarkation from the *Devonia,* a steam-ship of considerable tonnage. Maintaining the admittedly weak alias of Robert Stephenson, I clambered down the gangway at Castle Garden in the company of Mr Jones, the Welsh blacksmith and fellow traveller I had befriended during the course of the voyage. You would be hard-pressed to find a more uncomfortable crossing than we had experienced—the unsavoury food, the constant vomiting, the constipation, the incessant scratching, not to mention the haughty looks that the so-called "lords of the saloon" cast down upon those of us inhabiting the second cabins and steerage.

And yet our misery continued when, upon arriving in New York City that Sunday, the 17th of August in '79, we were greeted by a deluge that must have rivalled the downpour witnessed by Noah himself. Indeed, my entire stay, however brief, in the city nicknamed "Gotham" was accompanied by the steady drumbeat of falling water. No matter the discomfort or my desire to reach California as quickly as possible, I had to spend the night in the watery metropolis. There were no westward-bound railroads available to me that evening because the economical "emigrant trains" did not run on Sundays.

It had been raining when we docked, and the showers showed no sign of abating as we sought transportation to our digs. Though we had been warned aboard the *Devonia* about the New York City hucksters seeking to separate us from our money, we none the less paid dearly for spots on the soggy straw bottom of an open baggage wagon for the short ride from the docks to our lodgings.

It was still light at just past 6.00 that evening when our conveyance deposited us at Reunion House, the small establishment at No. 10 West Street advertised as presenting private rooms at low rates. To be sure, its location—just a few minutes' walk to the steamboat landing—was especially convenient. The following evening I would be sailing from that very dock the short distance across the Hudson River to Jersey City where I would board the train heading west. And yet owing to my financial duress, the low rates of Reunion House presented an even greater allure.

You should understand that problems with money plagued both Jones and me. Jones had been married and prosperous earlier in his life; but his wife had died, and his money had run out. As for me, my father—either disappointed in my failure to pursue a career in the law or disapproving of my current quest for love—had cut off my finances. Thus afflicted, Jones and I agreed to share a single room at twenty-five cents a night. With individual meals costing the same "two bits" (as the Americans call the quarter of a dollar), we exchanged nods and signed the register.

What a bargain we had struck! The bed was small enough to send me to the floor for sleeping. The other amenities—a solitary wooden chair and well-worn, wooden clothes-pegs for our wet coats—were not much better. In short, except for the not insignificant roof above our heads, we found no relief within our tiny cell from the dampness and gloom permeating the city that night. My skin itched, my lungs rattled, my teeth ached, my stomach growled (I still couldn't *sh*—) and now the walls appeared to be closing in.

Yet in spite of all this misery, I sensed that conditions had to improve. I took the time to remind myself that I had indeed reached the "promised land". I was in America, after all. My luck would have to turn. "O brave new world!" I reassured myself, *"post nubila Phoebus."* [After dark clouds, the sun.] Tomorrow would be a better day.

In the meantime, our melancholia persisted, a condition that did not go unrecognised by Michael Mitchell, the proprietor and publican of the Reunion. How often must he have encountered travellers like Jones and me, pilgrims who had suffered a ten-days' tumultuous voyage at sea and now faced the vagaries of life in New York City sodden with rain.

"Boys," said he, wiping clean some glasses at the bar, "I have just the remedy for your downcast spirits."

Expecting an offer of gin or rum or some other variety of alcohol on his shelf, I was duly surprised by his suggestion.

"What do you say to a night at the theatre? A British pantomime's going on this evening at Booth's. *Robinson Crusoe.* It's just the thing for wandering Brits. The theatre's at 23rd and 6th Avenue. It's a couple of miles from here; but even with all the rain, if you hurry, you should arrive just before the curtain goes up."

"Booth's?" I queried. It was the only word I had retained.

"*Edwin* Booth," Mitchell said with a nod, "the actor who built the theatre, *not* his goddam traitor of a brother you're probably thinking of—John Wilkes Booth who murdered Lincoln. Edwin's one of our greatest players."

The sensational has always interested me, and I confess to having cultivated a ghoulish curiosity in the Booth family since I had first learned of the President's assassination some fourteen years previous. Jones too expressed interest in seeing the place, yet our interests were quieted when Mitchell informed us that the theatre no longer belonged to brother Edwin.

"He couldn't make it work and lost the place to bankruptcy five years ago. As you can expect, the new owners wanted larger audiences. Oh, they continued to put on classical plays the way Booth did—you know, Shakespeare and the like—but to attract new people, they staged more crowd-friendly shows like these British pantomimes."

I was impressed with Mitchell. For an American, he displayed a keen sense of British Theatre. Within the world of *belles letters,* it was common knowledge that a great many Americans confused the word "pantomime" with the silent affair called "mime". But as I am certain Mitchell could attest, anyone who has ever attended a pantomime can tell you that, thanks to all the singing, joking, and—dare I say—participation from a spirited audience, the British "panto" is anything but silent.

In fact, most pantomimes—often inspired by popular children's tales like *Robin Hood* and *Aladdin*—take the original stories down a few pegs. You might expect the democratic audiences in America to demand more appearances of these irreverent productions; and yet the British pantomime remains a *rara avis* [rare bird] in the

States. If you believe *hôtelier* Mitchell, it is the desire to witness so uncommon a phenomenon that causes crowds to fill the local theatres when pantomimes are put on.

Thanks to current literary fashion, however, I was prodded by a more personal motivation. With narratives like *Robinson Crusoe,* Daniel Defoe's fictional account of the castaway sailor called Alexander Selkirk,[*] serving as inspiration, I myself had for some time been contemplating the composition of a sea adventure. That the panto version of *Robinson Crusoe* was being performed that very night was reason enough to see the show. No matter the cost of a ticket, visiting Booth's had just become my major objective for the evening.

All this I explained to my fellow-traveller Jones. With the promise that we would dine after the performance, I had every expectation that he would join me. After all, did each of us not consider himself the other's right-hand man? Such was the camaraderie we had cultivated aboard the *Devonia.* He moaned a bit about the cost of tickets; but when I suggested we could save money by walking to Booth's Theatre in the rain instead of hiring some sort of transport to take us there, he acquiesced. We stored our belongings in the room we had agreed to share—I, my knapsack, small valise, and railway-rug; Jones, his solitary travelling bag—pulled on our mackintoshes (mine over my favourite velveteen jacket), patted down on our flat caps, and gritted our teeth. Only then, armed with Mitchell's directions, did Jones and I emerge from Reunion House prepared to confront the elements.

---

[*] More recent scholarship has suggested Robert Knox, who lived as a captive on the island of Ceylon for nineteen years (1659-1678), as DeFoe's model. See Katherine Frank's *Crusoe: Daniel Defoe, Robert Knox and the Creation of a Myth.* (DDV)

How relentless the rain! It pelted us as we plodded along the flooded roadways. Massive buildings towered above, the odd awning or overhanging roof offering the most minimum of shelters. Gas lamps flickered in the rapidly falling darkness, the reflections of their light dancing in the wet and deserted sidewalks. No pushcarts, no vendors, no police interrupted the scene. The occasional hansom or carriage might roll past, but you did not have to be a native New Yorker to know that this evening was a time to remain indoors.

Lest it sound otherwise, let me reassure you that we did reach our destination just in time for the curtain's rise. Booth's Theatre itself was modern in its *accoutrements* and beautifully done up. Neither the darkness nor the rain could obscure the three towers rising above the mansard roof. Eager to escape the downpour, we quickly made our way into the foyer through one of the high-arched portals facing the street. Though the lobby smelled of sodden coats, the shiny marble floor remained continuously mopped. An imposing statue of Junius Brutus Booth, a distinguished Shakespearian performer as well as father to Edwin and John Wilkes, lorded over the scene.

On days less fouled by the weather, countless theatre-goers would have been mulling about the spacious lobby. As it was, we had no difficulty in locating the ticket window and purchasing inexpensive seats. Dashing to their location at the rear of the cavernous hall, Jones and I removed our coats. He sat down, but my hands began to itch again, and I scratched at them. Before I could take my seat, a cough racked through me, and I employed my right arm to cover my mouth.

Still, I did my best to settle into my chair. Even then, a chill coursed through my weakened body—I had already lost some fourteen pounds during the voyage—but, fortunately, I had my old skullcap to confound the cold, and I placed it atop my head moments before the overture began. Immediately, I felt improved. As if in sympathy, the sprightly music featured a gay tune or two, and I vowed to attempt them on my flageolet some day.

It was at the overture's end, with my maladies now in abeyance, that the curtain rose, and I caught my first glimpse of the actor William Escott. You should not believe that I focused my attention on that singular man during the entire performance. Yet in spite of all the pretty girls, menacing pirates, and diverting melodies, the way the one-legged Escott thumped about with a single crutch made him quite hard to miss.

It was in light of how the evening progressed, however, that I have chosen to concentrate my attention upon him at this point in my narrative. Although Jones and I came to learn the man's history only later that night, I believe that at the risk of upsetting the night's chronology, I should provide Escott's background before describing his performance. Such a detour should serve to help you navigate the troubling events that occurred following the play's conclusion.

*****

William Escott had begun his acting career in 1879 by joining the Shakespearian Company of Michael Sasanoff. And yet, though boasting of having performed with such theatrical giants as Sir Henry Irving and Sir Max Beerbohm Tree, Escott confessed to never having truly considered the stage as his calling. In point of fact, at age twenty-five, he had begun to envision his future not as an actor, but rather (in his own words) as a "consulting detective"—"the world's first," he hastened to add.

For Escott, acting served as necessary preparation. "There is no better way of penetrating a disguise," he announced, "than by being able to assume one." Without envisioning a theatrical career as his goal, he remained generally content—especially in the beginning—with small parts like the first or second "walking gentleman" or even "low comedian". For Escott, impersonation was the thing— learning the tricks of make-up and costume to appear convincingly in the persona of someone other that oneself.

In the early spring of '79, "Old Sasanoff" (as he was affectionately called by the actors) announced that he had arranged a lengthy tour of America for the troupe. Beginning in November, they were to spend a short time in New York City, proceed to Chicago, and then travel west. To Escott, such a trip posed more than the simple opportunity to further his acting skills. To him, the trip provided the perfect opportunity for familiarising himself with American life.

"I'd heard New York City described as 'The Modern Gomorrah', he told me, "and I wanted to know why. I needed more time there than Sasanoff was offering."

Although he never explained how he intended to go about it, Escott envisioned the metropolis as the perfect spot to examine the full range of criminal behaviours. As a consequence, having no central roles to perform in London, he asked Sasanoff if he might leave for America well before the others in the troupe and re-join them once they arrived in the fall. Apparently, Sasanoff liked Escott's work well enough to consent to the plan. Save for muttering about the need to find a replacement, Sasanoff agreed to rehire him upon reaching New York. In August, therefore, William Escott sailed off on his own for the United States.

Despite his inexpensive lodgings near Broadway, it did not take Escott long to consume most of the money he had set aside for his adventure; and he realised the need to find employment if he was to fend off starvation before November when the Sasanoff company was scheduled to arrive. As luck would have it, during a sightseeing venture to Booth's Theatre, he discovered that not only was a *Robinson Crusoe* panto about to be mounted there by the Watley players, a visiting group from England under the direction of Malcolm Watley, but also that the company stood in need of actors.

"*Robinson Crusoe* contains a number of stock characters," Escott explained, "the ship's crew, villagers, pirates, immortals, and the like—and the company required additional players to round out the large cast."

Upon seeing the advertisement, Escott applied to Watley himself and, thanks in equal parts to the actor's British upbringing and his theatrical experience, was immediately hired. In keeping with the tradition of the pantomime, his was a character that contained many parts— that of sea cook and pirate and one-legged man all rolled into one.

Silly though the panto may have been, it was thanks to that production of *Robinson Crusoe* that Escott learned how to contort not only his face, but also his body. To appear to be missing a limb, he was fitted with a leather, belt-like harness that kept his right-leg pulled up behind him. A long coat concealed this subterfuge, and Escott offered that it didn't take long to get used to hobbling about with the aid of the weathered crutch he was given to facilitate his movements. Although Escott said that he had actually come to like the illusion, he none the less admitted that once a performance ended, he had no hesitation in removing the harness and stretching out his liberated leg.

*****

Booth's Theatre provided us a brief respite from the weather, but not completely. At the performance Jones and I attended that Sunday evening, not only could you hear the rain pummelling the roof of the theatre, but you could also count the empty seats. And yet, as Lucretius tells us, *Ut quod ali cibus est aliis fuat acre venemum.* [One's man's meat is another man's poison.] Safely ensconced within the walls of a dry auditorium, Jones and I were not complaining. On the contrary, once the gaslights were turned down in the half-empty hall, we took the opportunity to improve our seating.

Replete with action, song, and dance, the performance offered much diversion. But through it all, the audience kept a collective eye on Escott. With a ridiculous wooden parrot of emerald green attached to his shoulder, the actor convincingly hobbled his way across the stage as pirate- ship's cook, eagerly flipping cloth pancakes into the air or uttering fierce growls while brandishing an ominous blade.

So fearsome an aspect did Escott project (in spite of the silly parrot) that members of the audience would shout out to warn the innocent Robinson Crusoe, "Hist! There he is!" "Be careful!" Such calls were particularly easy to distinguish in the half-filled auditorium; and Robinson Crusoe—played, in fact, by a young lady—would flit away in the nick of time. As a consequence, the sea-cook and the rest of the pirates, supposedly motivated by drink, broke into some sort of garbled song-and-laboured-dance about the evils they planned to perform the next time they caught up to Crusoe—something about fifteen sailors on a "dead man's chest" and a refrain of "yo ho ho and barrels of rum". Of course, the audience (what there was of it, at any rate) loved such antics.

As did Jones and I—so much so, in fact, that when the performance ended, I sent my card backstage—it contained my true name—to enquire if I might personally offer my appreciation to the actors. After all, it was not as if I was unknown in artistic circles. It was then that Jones learned my real name. Upon discovering that I was a recognised author, however, he offered no inclination to share the limelight and said he would await me in the lobby.

I learned later that it was William Escott who, upon hearing my name, had told the stage manager to allow me to join the actors. Apparently, Escott was able to identify me by dint of having attended a reading of mine at Hatchards; and after removing the harness and giving his previously hidden leg a few swings, he took the lead in introducing me to the rest of the company.

"Your panto was just the antidote I craved," said I to the assemblage of pirates, cannibals, and villagers. "I've been at sea for ten depressing days. I only just arrived this afternoon."

Scattered applause greeted my explanation.

"In fact, I'm leaving for California tomorrow."

"So soon?" someone said.

"What's in California?" asked another.

"Fanny Osbourne," I answered without thinking. "The woman I love."

Their collective warm-hearted sigh embraced me, and not a few female performers did the same. Some of the men patted me on the shoulder or even put an arm round my waist in congratulations. Yet people had their jobs to perform, and the stage-hands began moving props about in preparation for shutting down the set.

It took about a quarter-hour for the farewells to dissipate; but with the auditorium empty and the actors ready to leave, I offered my final compliments and began to move towards the exit and my meeting with Jones.

It was then that the trouble began.

*****

Reaching the wings to my left, I patted my pockets, as men are wont to do to check their contents. Suddenly, I stopped and began searching in earnest within all the pockets of my trousers, jacket and rain-coat.

"My wallet's missing!" I shouted. "My railway ticket is inside."

The players on the stage froze instantly. First there was chatter, and then there were people looking at the floor to see if the wallet had simply fallen out of my clothes. Following my directions, a uniformed usher still in the hall dashed to the rear of the theatre to the seats Jones and I had initially occupied and then to the seats we had later appropriated. In neither case did he find any sign of the missing billfold.

Watley muttered something about sending for the police; but Escott, harbouring a gleam in his grey eyes, immediately spoke up.

"Let's try solving this problem on our own," said he. "We don't need the authorities to settle the matter."

Watley furrowed his brow, but he said nothing. Escott took the expression as one of approval and immediately directed the stage-hands to commandeer the exits so no one could leave the stage. He then asked all the actors to assemble before the scrim. How strange to see the *dramatis personae* [characters in a play] posed in front of a background depicting the shingle of a deserted island. Some had already donned their street clothes; and even I, untutored sleuth that I was, could understand that a trip to the changing rooms provided an opportunity for hiding the pilfered billfold, a supposition that provoked Escott to request that a pair of stage-hands search the dressing areas. Yet it was apparent from his lack of interest in their investigations that the actor believed anyone trying to make off with the wallet would more than likely still have it on his person in order to facilitate a quick escape.

At the same time Escott began manoeuvring people about, my friend Jones reappeared from the lobby through a rear door. My outburst had obviously summoned him back. You must know that while I never considered him capable of theft, I was pleased that his absence from the stage ruled him out as a suspect. Even now he displayed the common sense to occupy a seat at the rear of the auditorium and not become involved in the confusion at the front. On the contrary, I do believe he understood that yet another stage performance—a more serious production—was about to begin, and he wanted to watch the new scene develop.

"I suggest, Mr Watley," Escott said, "that we begin by searching the group. We might ask Miss Ross to conduct the service for the women. Her Crusoe costume is so form-fitting that it precludes any opportunity for hiding away a billfold."

The young woman blushed, but proceeded to assemble the other females in the cast. Escott himself motioned for the men to group together. In retrospect, such actions must have been a diversion. For after Escott had looked one particular man over from head to toe, Escott placed his arm about the man's shoulders and ushered him to centre stage. It seemed obvious that the amateur detective had reached a preliminary conclusion.

James Flint had exchanged his pirate's costume for tweed coat and trousers and was carrying a rain-coat in preparation for departing. With high, chiselled cheekbones, a strong chin, flashing eyes, and luxuriant black hair, he possessed many of the features required for major roles. But standing barely five feet high, he remained too short.

"Mr Flint," said Escott, "might we check your pockets? You—"

Before Escott could say anymore, the actor laid his mac on a chair and pulled a brown-leather billfold from inside his coat. With a mocking grin, he announced, "Just my own wallet," and he held it high in the air for all to see.

Escott looked at me questioningly.

"Mine's black," said I, shaking my head.

"Let's see what your other pockets hold."

Flint made a show of turning out all his pockets, including those in the cast-aside rain-coat, maintaining his grin all the while.

But Escott was not to be denied. With the silly wooden parrot flopping on his shoulder, he turned and began to stride uphill to the back of the stage on a floor raked about five degrees. The rest of the company followed; and after some ten steps, he halted before a six-foot-square trap door, the onstage egress to the storage or trap room below the boards, an area called the "cellarage". It was through just such an opening that "bodies" were seen to be buried and ghosts to magically rise.

"Here!" Escott announced, pointing downward with his long forefinger. His eyes were shining, and his cheeks were tinged pink. But only for a moment.

Just as Escott had bent forward, Flint leapt upon him from behind, knocking the parrot to the stage in the process. The villain was grasping a fearsome knife and, holding his hand low, brought the six inches of flashing steel up into Escott's chest. I myself witnessed the knife pushed in all the way to the hilt, a thrust that could not have failed to penetrate poor Escott's heart.

*****

With screams and shouts filling the auditorium, a burly stage-hand grabbed Flint and pulled him away from Escott. The knife clattered to the floor, and I expected to see gouts of blood gush from Escott's chest. Instead, he rose to his feet and with the calmest of demeanours faced a circle of wide eyes and raised brows.

"You—you're all right then, William?" Nelly asked. "How can that be? I saw the knife enter your body."

Hushed voices and bobbing heads reflected the concerns of the entire troupe.

"Sleight of hand," Escott explained with a dry chuckle. "I suspected Flint from the start. He was already dressed and too eager to leave. I was able to check his pockets for the missing wallet when I escorted him to centre-stage. Though I felt no wallet but the one he displayed, I did detect an unseen dagger tucked into his belt. It was mere child's play to replace the real item with the retractable-bladed knife that still resided in my own pocket. Flint acted so quickly against me that he had no chance to note the switch."

Flint struggled all the more mightily to free himself—fortunately, to no avail.

"I can only assume," Escott went on, "that such reckless behavior confirms his guilt. Shall we see?"

Escott now stood about a foot downstage from the trap door amidst the sawdust employed to represent sand. So positioned, he fell to his knees and, raising the trap door, crawled round its frame, running his fingers along the wooden moulding just inside the cavity. He obviously believed that the recess served as a cache for the stolen wallet.

"Bah!" Escott shouted in frustration. Having discovered nothing secreted within the woodwork, he searched again—still to no avail. "It *has* to be here," I heard him mutter just before he jumped down into the trap room itself. Moments later, the under-stage room took on a yellow glow; he had obviously found a lantern.

I moved close enough to the opening to see a few of the treasures below—a small oaken table, a discarded tree of *papier- mâché*, a furled red flag leaning against the back wall. I caught a glimpse of Escott as well. Ignoring the slight stoop, there was just enough room for him to stand. Then suddenly the light extinguished. "No need for a thorough search here," he announced in a voice muffled by the below-stage enclosure. "Flint didn't have enough time to be too clever."

Curiously enough, though Escott climbed out empty-handed, a look of genuine surprise appeared on Flint's face. Almost immediately, however, it transformed into a self-satisfied smirk.

"No wallet, eh, Escott?" he declaimed, squirming in the arms of the man who was holding him. Flint might have been orating in the midst of a play. "May I ask why you thought it was *I* who took it? Why you felt you could besmirch my good name in front of my colleagues?"

Escott looked momentarily puzzled. "I thought it was obvious, Mr Flint," said he at last. "In the world of detection there is much to be learned from trouser knees. Yours, sir, are flecked with bits of sawdust, sawdust precisely the same as that scattered on the floor near the trap door. Anyone can see that you were on your knees by the opening."

The stage-hand released his grip, and immediately Flint brushed the legs of his trousers clean. "Proves nothing, does it?" said he.

Escott's eyes now turned back to the assembled actors. Slowly, he scrutinised the appearances of them all. He seemed to be seeking out another thief. *Incidis in Scyllam cupiens vitare Charybdim.* [From the frying pan into the fire.] If he could not produce an alternative culprit, I assumed that he and the young actress would have to search the entire group.

Suddenly, Escott turned to face a white-bearded fellow identified by Watley as Bennie Gunn, the actor who had played a shipwrecked old sailor. He was still dressed in his costume of heavy blue cotton trousers and billowing white shirt.

"Do you mind, Mr Gunn?" Escott asked.

Gunn looked quizzical as Escott examined the man's shirtsleeves. Even I could detect the dark stains at the right cuff, which Escott was just then sniffing.

"Darjeeling, I should judge," Escott observed.

Immediately, Gunn pulled his arm back and sprang for the small stairway downstage that led into the auditorium and the exit. At that same moment, I saw my friend Jones rise in the back of the hall though I could not fathom what he might do if Gunn were actually to confront him. But the actor never even reached the stairs. Another of the stage-hands blocked his escape, grabbing him round his upper arms.

*****

Escott made his way to the wings where a dull brass samovar stood on a table. "This container," said he, resting his palm on the metal lid, "is filled with tea before every performance and is generally tapped out by the end." So saying, he carefully raised the lid, peered inside, and nodded. "Dry," he announced, "but not completely empty." He proceeded to thrust his hand inside and to pluck out a black leather wallet, which he held up for all to see.

"That's it!" I cried, dashing towards him. "That's mine. You can see my tickets inside—though not much else."

Indeed, there were but a couple of dollars within— little enough to attract a thief. But then a thief cannot detect a wallet's contents in advance. Escott also produced my ticket for the next day's evening-ferry to Jersey City as well as my railway ticket for travel from thence to San Francisco and even my cancelled ticket from the ship *Devonia*. There could be no doubt that the billfold was mine.

"Well done, Escott," said I as he handed it over. To the actor's great embarrassment, the entire theatre company broke into applause.

"You may have found the wallet," snarled Gunn, "but you can't prove it was I who stole it."

"I mentioned trouser-knees before, did I not?" Escott replied. "In my eagerness to confront Flint, I neglected to mention the equally important cuffs of shirtsleeves. There is much to be learned from them as well. It was Flint who initially pickpocketed the wallet and placed it beneath the trap door. But it was Gunn who, having watched all this transpire, removed the wallet from Flint's hiding place and hid it in the now-empty samovar—though not carefully enough to prevent some errant tea from staining his right-sleeve cuff. I have no doubt that after removing his costume, he would have gone straight to the samovar to retrieve his booty."

Watley now took command of his company, issuing orders to the stage-hands regarding Gunn and Flint: "Throw them out! The both of them. Take them to the alley in the back."

Grabbing the thieves by the shoulders, the big men shoved the two through the wings and to the rear of the theatre. Moments later, we heard a door open and the rush of falling rain. Cold air accompanied by a wet smell wafted onto the stage. Then there were the thuds of bodies being struck and the slam of the door.

"Well done, sir!" Watley crowed, slapping Escott on the back. "Well done, indeed! No need for the police when William Escott is present, eh?"

Amidst a final cascade of compliments, the members of the cast began to disperse. The moment offered me the opportunity to express my own appreciation.

"I'd like to thank you, Mr Escott," I said. "Perhaps you would honour me as a my guest for a late-night dinner. If you can recommend a place within my meagre means, I would be happy to host you."

Escott clasped my hand. "I would be more than happy to spend the time with you, sir," said he, "but there's no need for you to go to any such expense. I shall pay my own way."

I am rather afraid that a blush crossed my face, and I nervously scratched at my hands. This clever fellow had clearly noted the economical status of my travel tickets—the second-class cabin arrangements aboard the *Devonia* and the seat aboard one of the infamous "emigrant trains". Everyone knew that such a railway was devised to convey the newly arrived—and therefore the most frugal of travellers—westward in the least expensive manner. Yet if Escott recognised that my claim to literary recognition had so far produced no outward signs of monetary success, he kept silent on the matter.

"My father," I said and explained to him my financial predicament."

"We each must follow our own paths, Mr Stephenson," Escott observed.

The actor requested a few minutes to exchange his sea-cook's costume for more traditional garb. He soon reappeared, and after once again being congratulated by the remaining members of the troupe, he donned his mackintosh and soft cloth cap, a unique affair with bills in front and back and earflaps that tied together at the top. Jones and I put on our own rain-coats and flat caps and, thus prepared to face the drenched streets of New York City, set out to find a restaurant that fit my requirements.

*****

Escott guided us to a French establishment not far from the theatre. Happily, it took but a glance at the bill of fare to assure me that the restaurant would fulfil not only my culinary desires but my financial requirements as well. With my skullcap safely secured atop my head again, I eagerly joined Escott and Jones in a most satisfactory repast. It was during this meal that Escott reported to us the facts concerning his life that I presented to you earlier—the details of his acting career, his visit to Hatchards, his trip to New York City, and his interest in becoming a consulting detective.

Even if the wine and chicken did not pass for authentic *coq au vin,* I must say that in light of all the challenging events of the day, it was quite the feast. Yet to be honest, I was most appreciative of the coffee. The wretched brew on the ship had tasted of snuff; indeed, you could scarcely tell it apart from the tea.

Following dinner, we shared cigarettes—I rolled my favourite Three Castles—and after a few puffs began to cough.

Both Escott and Jones showed signs of concern as my hacking went on. But I waved them off with a few flicks of my hand.

"Not to worry," I told my companions and immediately changed the subject. "You know of my scribbling," I said to Escott. "I'm hoping to produce a narrative of this trip worthy of publication."

My new friends both raised their glasses.

"To your next work," said the actor.

I smiled, appreciative of Escott's support. In point of fact, I had been elaborating the plans for my sea story that very evening as I watched Escott hopping about on stage. The affair with the wallet had simply put it out of mind.

Now, however, I felt ready to announce my intention. "Escott," I said, "for some time now, I've been mulling over the idea for a sea-faring adventure tale; and I owe it to you that—no matter what happens during my journey west—I'm actually going to begin the thing."

The actor cocked an eyebrow.

"No, really, Escott, your portrayal of the one-legged sea cook inspired me. The crutch. The parrot. And later, when you uncovered that empty hidey-hole below the stage. It's all helped me move the plot along—as, indeed, have some of the colourful names I heard tonight."

Escott shrugged. "Glad to be of service," said he, clinking his glass with mine.

A chuckle escaped my lips. "I expect that people are going to say that my hobbled pirate was modelled after my one-legged friend, the poet William Henley. I must admit that, thanks to him, writing a story about someone so afflicted had crossed my mind. But *your* performance—not to mention that wobbly parrot—seems to have been just the inspiration I needed to touch off the action. And for that I am truly grateful."

Escott sat silently staring at me for a few moments. There are those who say that my widely-set eyes cause people to become meditative. Whatever his motivation, he seemed to be contemplating his next words carefully. Finally, he gave a brief nod, as if indicating to himself that he had decided in the affirmative. "Speaking of role-playing, " said he, "you should know that William Escott is not my real name; it is my acting pseudonym. In reality, I am called Sherlock Holmes."

In the Bohemian world of theatre, such news caused no great excitement. "Well then," said I, "here's to Sherlock Holmes," and I raised my glass. "Call me 'Louis'," I added with a smile.

"I'm still Jones," chuckled the third member of our group.

Jones had always known me as "Robert" and must have wondered if all of us artistic types—indeed, all of humanity—harboured dual identities. I know I contemplated the question. I should imagine, for instance, that few members of the Watley Company realised that the calm exteriors of James Flint and Bennie Gunn concealed the hearts of thieves. Actors were trained to hide their true natures. We were in America at the time, so I offer you Wilkes Booth as the pre-eminent example.

We finished our smokes, and Escott walked Jones and me back through the rain to Reunion House. The showers were not as heavy as earlier in the day, but the rain was still coming down in watery curtains. The next evening I would begin my long railway excursion to the west. I had no reason to think that I would ever again hear the name Sherlock Holmes. But at least I could complete this part of my journey in the belief that, however inadvertently, I might have played some small role in helping forge the career of the world's first consulting detective.

III

The day after I had read Stevenson's narrative, I made my way to the London Library in St. James's Square. It was there that the sub-librarian Lomax procured for me a copy of the very novel whose creation had been triggered by Stevenson's visit to the panto at Booth's Theatre. Book in hand, I proceeded to the Northumberland Arms near Trafalgar Square. My literary agent, Arthur Conan Doyle, and I had scheduled a holiday meeting at one of his favourite public houses to discuss my idea for a story about Holmes's recent return to life. (It had been just a few months since Holmes had shocked me with his dramatic re-appearance following his encounter with Professor Moriarty at the

Reichenbach Falls—"shocking" since Holmes had been thought dead for close to three years.) As Conan Doyle and I exchanged literary strategies, we also enjoyed a tankard or two. Conan Doyle paused, however, when he noted the book at my side.

"The late Robert Louis Stevenson, I see," he observed grimly. "What a loss. Another Scotsman with genius—a wonderful teller of tales. If I do say so myself, Louis was one of the great storytellers of the race. He glorified the 'masculine type', if you take my meaning. Do you know that there are those who call that book next to you the finest narrative in the English language? He wrote it in the two years following his meeting with Holmes—no doubt the reason for originally titling it 'The Sea Cook". Louis himself employed the pseudonym of Captain George North and first published the thing in serialised sections in the children's magazine called Young Folks. The rest, as they say, is history."

Conan Doyle paused to sample the ale. Then, almost as an afterthought, he added, "Do you know, John, that way back in April of '83, not long after The Sea Cook had appeared, Louis wrote to me just how much he enjoyed Sherlock Holmes? To tell the truth, I didn't know if he meant the man himself or the hero of your accounts—though he did say that reading one of your stories had given him momentary relief from a bout of pleurisy."

My agent broke into a round of hearty laughter. "As a doctor myself," he said, "I regard that as quite a compliment. Don't you agree?"

I nodded sadly, thinking of Stevenson's early death.

Later that evening, following a meal of lamb and potatoes excellently prepared by Mrs Hudson, I settled into my armchair in the sitting room with the book in my hands.

Holmes's tin box and the Stevenson manuscript were no longer in sight. A fire crackled in the hearth, and I prepared myself for a relaxing read. With Christmas but a week away, 221B seemed the most ideal spot in the world.

With a satisfied smile, I opened the book called Treasure Island. *In no less than three pages, I encountered young Jim Hawkins and the Admiral Benbow Inn and Billy Bones, the fierce-looking sailor with the sabre cut on his cheek. It was Bones who warned the lad to keep his "weather-eye open for a sea-faring man with one leg . . . ."*

The Adventure of the Second William Wilson

The mask and mantle of the unknown drop off, and Alfonso
discovers his own image, —the spectre of himself.
--Washington Irving
"An Unwritten Drama of
Lord Byron"

Straightway the door opened, and a shrivelled, shabby dwarf
entered . . . . This vile bit of human rubbish seemed to bear a sort
of remote and ill-defined resemblance to me.
--Mark Twain
"The Facts Concerning
the Recent Carnival of Crime
in Connecticut"

*O*ne cannot play a role in the detecting business—let
alone *write* of the profession—without harbouring an opinion
on the subject of Edgar Allan Poe.   The American author so
often referred to as "The Father of the Detective Story"
evokes strong reactions in all kinds of readers, but especially
in those directly connected to criminal investigations.
Sherlock Holmes himself was not immune to Poe's sway.
And yet for so clear a thinker as Holmes, his views on Poe's
crime-solving skills were known to waver.

As much as he might deny it, my logical-thinking
friend had always been of two minds regarding the writer. At
the start of his career, Holmes appeared to look down upon
the man. In our first investigation together, the account of

which I titled *A Study in Scarlet*, he labelled Poe's fictional detective "a very inferior fellow".

"You should note, Watson," Holmes said, "C. Auguste Dupin is by no means the phenomenon Poe imagined him to be."

But Holmes also harboured another opinion. In a later case, an investigation I called "The Cardboard Box", he praised Dupin as a "close reasoner"—not unlike himself. Never comfortable with reversals of opinion, however, Holmes duly suggested that it was I, not he, who had initially doubted Dupin's credibility.

Though it is an easy matter for me to plead not guilty to such unfair charges, my faithful readers need not accept my pledge of innocence on its own. Events themselves offer corroborating evidence. In late 1882, the details of a strange new case forced Holmes to confront both sides of his conflicted attitude towards Poe. It required no less than a gruesome crime to cause Sherlock Holmes to question the dichotomy between Poe's celebrated psychological insight and the writer's equally renowned literary flights of fancy.

*****

Poe himself would have appreciated the beginnings of the matter. It was a dark Monday evening in a suitably bleak and dreary December, when Billy the Page came suddenly rapping at our chamber door.

"Enter!" Holmes called, and Billy stepped inside.

Holmes and I rose as the lad adjusted his livery and announced, "Mr William Wilson."

Directly behind Billy came a distinguished-looking gentleman. Dressed in a bespoke dark suit that contrasted nicely with his grey side-whiskers, he maintained a fine head of black hair combed straight back. Yet in spite of his august appearance, he had the unusual habit of constantly glancing round our sitting room. His blue eyes darted everywhere—peering beyond the chairs and tables, examining the windows, looking backward at the door, which Billy had closed upon exiting.

I judged him an obvious paranoiac, demonstrably worried that he had been followed. Indeed, he went so far as to check that the door latch had been secured. After assuring himself that all was in order, he began bouncing his gaze back and forth between my friend and me.

"Mr Holmes?" he asked.

"I am Sherlock Holmes," said my companion. Gesturing in my direction, he added, "This is my friend and colleague, Dr Watson. Whatever you have to say to me, you may say to him as well."

"I am called William Wilson," came the reply. "It is a name with which you might be familiar."

Holmes cocked an eyebrow.

"From the story with that title by Edgar Allan Poe," the man added.

It took me a moment to recall the piece. Once I did, I wondered how the man dared to identify himself so definitively. It is always dangerous to trust one of Poe's narrators; but if I remembered correctly, the storyteller states that so abhorrent is the tale he is about to relate that he fears sullying the "fair page" with his "real appellation". In light of our visitor's claim, one had to question whether the storyteller's denial was a ruse, or whether our guest was guilty of a ridiculous charade.

"I know the story," said I coldly. "I'm sure Mr Holmes does as well."

"Indeed I do," said my friend with a nod. "It is a difficult story to forget. The aforementioned William Wilson encounters someone he believes looks and sounds just like himself—an intriguing mirror-image the Germans term a *Doppelgänger*. This alter ego, who even bears the same name as William Wilson, follows Wilson to the Carnival in Rome. Driven mad by the constant pursuit, Wilson employs the rapier that is part of his costume to stab his double to death. Or so it appears."

Leave it to Holmes to hit exactly the right mark with his ambiguity. For as I then remembered, it is in a conclusion left open to interpretation that renders the entire story so perplexing. Through literary sleight of hand, Poe forces the reader to question whether Wilson, rather than having killed some evil tormentor, has in reality viewed himself in a mirror—a mirror that might or might not exist—and inflicted the bloody wounds upon his own person.

"What relationship does the story have to *you*?" Holmes asked our visitor.

The man stood tall. "The original William Wilson was my father."

"Preposterous!" I cried. "The story is mere fiction."

The visitor shook his head. "Gentlemen," said he with a dry chuckle, "I can assure you that you are mistaken. Neither is the story untrue—nor am I mad.'"

"You present a singular situation, sir," said Holmes, reaching for his favourite briar. "I'm certain I speak for Dr Watson when I say we wish to hear you out."

Stifling my scepticism, I muttered some words of agreement. At the same time, Holmes indicated that our visitor take a seat. The man calling himself William Wilson did just that, and Holmes and I occupied armchairs opposite his. "Now," said my friend as he filled his pipe, "pray, explain yourself."

Wilson took a deep breath. "As you are doubtlessly aware," he began, "Edgar Allan Poe was born in America. John and Frances Allan, the people who took him in following his father's abandonment and his mother's early death, brought him to England at a young age."

"To Stoke Newington, was it not?" Holmes asked as he lit his pipe.

"Quite right. They settled in the picturesque village just north of London. Poe's biographers will tell you that the hamlet described in his narrative about William Wilson was based on that very locale right down to the thick, cloying mist and the massive, twisted trees. For that matter, Bransby, the headmaster of young William's prison-like school in the story, bears the same name as the headmaster of the school attended by Poe himself."

Tenuous proof, I remember thinking at the time. *Poe may simply have liked the name.*

"I provide this information, gentlemen, to enable you to make the leap that literary critics seem so unwilling to perform—that is, to accept as fact a supposedly fictional story, however bizarre. Poe was describing the actual location where, as a youth, he had befriended a real lad he called William Wilson. As a consequence, I implore you to recognise the narrative in question not as a mere fabrication but rather as a true chronicle of past events."

Holmes's response to this singular request was to exhale a cloud of blue smoke towards the ceiling. I, on the other hand, confess to experiencing a degree of sympathy. After all, to this very day, my own accounts of the true exploits of Sherlock Holmes continue to be misidentified as fiction.

"To their delight," Wilson resumed, undaunted by Holmes's indifferent reaction, "the boys discovered they shared the same birthday; and soon thereafter they became fast friends. Once Poe returned to America a few years later, the youths began a correspondence that continued into manhood.

"Poe's letters are gone now; but being the wordsmith that he was, he recognised not only the attraction of the details Wilson recounted in his letters, but also the reckless abandon with which he described them. There seems little doubt that Wilson too appreciated what he himself had written. We'll never know the precise reason, of course, but presumably some dubious promise of anonymity from Poe prompted William to grant his friend permission to convert the many letters into a single, factual narrative."

Holmes allowed another cloud of smoke to escape his lips.

"You have read," our visitor continued, "of Wilson's attendance at Oxford and his intemperate behaviour there."

"In particular," I felt compelled to add, "his involvement with licentious women."

"'Profligacy'," stated Holmes, the pipe clenched in his teeth. "'Miserable profligacy' is the phrase employed by Poe."

"Quite right," said the man. "'Miserable profligacy' is exactly the term. So is 'debaucheries'. He used others as well—'soulless dissipation' and 'dangerous seductions' to name two more. I can assure you that such demeaning language most accurately describes his foul actions."

"You seem to speak from experience," I observed drily.

Our visitor smiled. "No, Dr Watson, I wish the answer was that simple. You see, gentlemen, much as it grieves me to report the fact, my own mother, whom I loved very much, was one of those young whores who serviced Wilson and his chums."

"Good heavens!" I cried. "One doesn't usually hear a gentleman speak so rudely of his own mother."

"I note," said Holmes coldly, "that you refer to the woman in the past tense. May we assume that she has died?"

"Yes, Mr Holmes. She died a few weeks ago at age seventy-two."

"A ripe old age," I observed.

"To be sure, Doctor; and yet the longer she lived, the more she feared going to her grave without providing me with the truth about my birth. I am no student of literature, you see, and had no cause to be familiar with the writings of Mr Poe. I can assure you that his works occupied no place on the shelves in our home. This last fact was the primary reason for my surprise when after her death. I discovered that my mother had left me an anthology of Poe's stories. Needless to say, it included Poe's account of William Wilson—along with a letter from my mother that explained the story's significance.'

"A letter, you say? Do you have it with you?"

"Yes, Mr Holmes. I thought that you would want to see it."

Sherlock Holmes extended his long fingers in anticipation whilst Wilson withdrew a set of folded papers from an inner pocket and placed them in Holmes's open palm. My friend proceeded to read the missive and then passed the pages to me. Here is the letter that we read:

10 October 1882

My Dearest William,

By the time you read this, I shall be gone, happy to face a better world, but happier still to know I have left you comfortable in this one. I cannot move on in peace, however, without providing you with specific knowledge of your own peculiar background. For all your lifetime I have been fearful of telling you your history, but during every one of those years my silence has gnawed at me. I cannot deprive you any longer of the knowledge of your past. No parent likes to advertise the misdeeds of their youth or to describe for their children the crumbling foundation upon which a false family history has been constructed. Yet I find myself in precisely that situation. Just as I confront my own fate, I cannot turn away from showing you yours.

You know of my early youth. Although my mother died in childbirth, I was brought up in a proper home in Gloucestershire. My father—your grandfather—was a vicar and provided me with an education. But I found such a simple life unappealing; and thanks in great part to my comely appearance, I came to believe at a youthful age that I might travel to Oxford and find some rising young man who could provide me not only with a family, but also with a material improvement in my fortune.

Sadly, difficult though it is to admit, I was taken advantage of. As a result, my dreams faded. I lost hope in securing a suitable man to be my husband—and yet I could never ignore the appeal of lucre. On the contrary, my lust for riches continued to grow. In short, though I hesitate to write the words, I spent most of my evenings in the arms of young men who sought nothing more than paying for all manner of delights of the flesh. Needless to say, amidst words of righteous indignation, my father, your grandfather, abandoned me.

My reputation as a bewitching temptress brought me gold and infamy, and it was not long before I met one William Wilson, a debauched young man with lots of money. Inflicting pain and humiliation were his chief desires, and he seemed intent on fulfilling his wants. In a word, he appeared a ruthless master. It was only later that I discovered the inner torment he suffered. He claimed to fear the vengeance of some sort of evil twin, a double that he said had haunted him from their first encounter years before. On occasion, he would whisper that I should run away. But no sooner did he dismiss me than he would cry out for protection from the devilish creature that was driving him mad. The longer I knew your father, the more I heard him rant and rave, and yet I assure you that no such phantom ever showed itself to me.

But why dwell upon the macabre?

You can read of his horrific escapades and nightmares yourself in the story by Mr Poe that bears your father's name. As for the two of us, William and I remained together until I discovered I was with child. When I told him I would not rid myself of it—of you—*he wanted nothing more to do with me. Not even Mr Poe, famous for his tales of the depraved, could bring himself to include my tragic chapter in his own history of William Wilson.*

And yet I must give the devil his due. Thanks to the largess of his parents, William was awash with money, and— quite the cheat at Écarté—raised his own small pile at the gaming tables. As a result, he was willing enough to supply me with enough funds to live quite comfortably during my confinement. He required but two conditions. I was to give my child his *name (if I was lucky enough to have a son), and I was never to reveal the source of my income. I am pleased to say that the fund was generous enough to allow me and you (for you were, indeed, the son I was blessed to have) to live comfortably. Happily, the money was sufficient for me to send you to school even after William's death. To spare you the pain, I invented all that business about a military father who had served his country nobly and died in battle. Although secrecy no longer matters, not even when you came of age did I have the courage to inflict upon you the ugly truth of your conception. That you have become a solicitor with a successful practice could make no mother more proud.*

Though I have said that your father, despite his latent cruelty, could never bring himself to completely forsake his former mistress and his son, neither did he ever wish to see us again. So utterly damning did I find his rejection that I began to fear that you, my only child, might have inherited some aspect of his deeply distorted nature. That is why I never encouraged you to marry or to start a family of your own, but rather to stay by me and care for your aging mother. Read the words of Mr Poe to understand your awful beginnings. Even as my time on earth draws to a close, you must become aware of the hidden dangers lurking within your soul; they threaten every fibre of your being.

Take heed and avoid the fate of your father.

It was signed, "Your adoring mother."

After I had finished reading the letter, Holmes addressed Mr Wilson: "With all due respect to the deceased, one cannot treat the account of an illusory *Doppelgänger* as Truth. Even your mother, the authoress of this fable, admits that she never saw the alleged simulacrum, that she had only read Poe's account of it. Not to speak ill of the dead, sir, but perhaps your mother had become delusional towards the end of a very long life."

80

Our visitor nodded. "So I thought too, Mr Holmes; and following her death, I read Poe's story just as she had instructed. Though the plot substantiated many of the events described in her letter—and, by the same token, made me question the basic touchstones of my life—what else could I do but consider her fears the ravings of a demented mind? I continued to doubt her warnings—continued doubting until a week ago. That was when I saw him."

"Saw *whom*?" I asked.

Wilson ran a hand through his thick black hair. "I know you will find this hard to believe, gentlemen," said he. "In fact, I fully expect you to resort to all the predictable explanations—delusion, dream, hallucination. But as I sit here now in Baker Street, so last week did I see a man who looked very much like me—very much indeed. He's followed me to and from work for most of the last few days. Sometimes he waits across the road from my club to dog my heels. When I attended the opera last week, I saw him lurking in the shadows of Covent Garden. And always, he follows me home. On one occasion, he got close enough to whisper my name."

Sherlock Holmes showed his teeth in what can only be described as a condescending smile. "I must confess, Mr Wilson, that your situation prompts my curiosity; yet I must also caution that in no way should my interest cause you to assume my belief in your imaginings."

Our visitor's face flushed. "See here, Mr Holmes, I'm willing to pay you to look into this affair. The police are not interested."

"I should think not. I doubt the name Poe means anything to the Yarders—let alone the name William Wilson. But though your case warrants attention and you have come to the right place to register your fears, I make no promises about how any such investigation may be resolved."

"But you *will* look into the matter, Mr Holmes? You *will* uncover whoever or whatever it is that tracks me? I shall go mad if you turn me down."

Holmes placed his pipe in a nearby ashtray. "The addresses of your chambers and rooms, if you please," said he, offering Wilson a sheet of paper and pencil. "Give it to Dr Watson."

Wilson scribbled the information about his rooms near Long Acre Street and his law office at the Inns of Court. He handed the paper to me, and in exchange Holmes gave him one of his visiting cards upon which he had written his fee. Wilson nodded his approval and thanked us both.

"One final question, Mr Wilson," said Holmes as he opened the door.

Wilson turned to face him.

"I must ask if you have recently committed some 'folly of vice'?"

"I beg your pardon," said Wilson.

"A folly of vice—the expression employed by Poe to describe an immoral act. Such behaviour on your part might have summonsed your father's double. A less-discerning critic might call that double a conscience."

"I-I should say not," replied Wilson with a bit of hesitation. Seemingly uncertain about the merits of his response, he walked hesitantly out of our sitting room and down the stairs.

Once Holmes heard the outer door close, he moved to the window and drew back the white curtain.

"From this vantage," said he, still facing the glass, "it would appear that no one is following our Mr Wilson. Tomorrow, however, we shall investigate more thoroughly."

Holmes settled back into the armchair. Steepling his fingers and narrowing his eyes, he observed, "If Wilson's tale is accurate, we are in deep waters, old fellow. Tomorrow, we shall put to the test the question that underlies Wilson's story: was Edgar Poe merely inventing diversions or was he, in fact—as our client seems to believe—relating a frightening historical truth."

I nodded. Holmes's own conflicting views of the American writer could not have been expressed more clearly.

*****

I came down to breakfast the next morning expecting to find Holmes at table. Instead, I encountered an officious, grey-haired fellow with a clipped painter's-brush moustache. He was dressed in dark-blue kepi and uniform and seemed to be inspecting the gas lines leading to our light fixtures.

"May I help you, sir?" I asked rather sharply, wondering why Mrs Hudson would let so offensive a personage into our rooms without first gaining our permission—unless, of course, it was Holmes himself who had admitted him. But there was no sign of my friend, and the Inspector had moved from examining the pipelines to rearranging some of Holmes's laboratory equipment.

"I say, take your hands off that test tube," I commanded.

"I'm simply trying—" the intruder attempted to explain in a high-pitched voice.

"Nevermore!" I interrupted, surprised at how easily a refrain from Poe had crept into my vocabulary.

"Why, Dr Watson," the man squeaked, "cannot a fellow"—and suddenly his voice became more familiar—"move about his own paraphernalia?"

The inspector, of course, was Sherlock Holmes, and I had been taken in. I looked to the heavens for solace.

"A test, Watson. If I can fool you, I should easily be able to fool someone who does not know me at all, eh?"

"And what sort of costume are you in today?"

"I am whatever kind of inspector I need to be. I shall follow Mr Wilson from a distance, stopping when necessary to examine whatever is close by—metal pipes, street lamps, broken window glass—whatever causes no commotion by having a uniformed person like myself scrutinizing it. In such a manner, I should be able to blend into the scenery."

"And I? What am I to do?"

"As you are not an early riser and also have your patients to attend in the morning, I thought that you might follow Wilson home from work."

I nodded in agreement. "And do you have a disguise for me to wear?"

"No need," Holmes chuckled. "Just wear your usual dark suit and bowler, and you will look like all the barristers and solicitors running about the Inns of Court. No one will notice you."

With a wave, he was off; and I, before setting off for my surgery, was free to sit down with a breakfast of Mrs Hudson's eggs and ham.

*****

Wilson's law chambers were located just beyond Lincoln's Inn Fields, the large square laid about by Inigo Jones in the seventeenth century. In spite of the dark clouds that afternoon, it seemed safe enough to eschew a hansom; and as I walked the two miles from our rooms to the very centre of the British legal system, I found no need to open my umbrella.

Sherlock Holmes correctly predicted that, dressed in a dark suit and bowler, I would blend in with the similarly attired barristers, solicitors, benchers, and clerks parading through the Inns of Court. On grey days like the one in question, even my furled brolly appeared *de rigueur*.

Fortunately, I had no difficulty locating the redbrick Georgian building whose address Wilson had provided; and beneath a plane tree near the green, I found a wooden bench to sit upon whilst waiting for the man himself to appear.

The December night fell quickly, yet I had no problem discerning Wilson's distinctive black mane beneath his bowler as he exited his chambers. Indistinguishable from the legal types surrounding me, I trailed after him at a safe distance along the narrow, gas-lit confines of Bell Yard on the way to the Strand. As Wilson had done during his visit to Baker Street, he would frequently turn his head in all manner of directions, presumably in search of someone seeking him harm. I had no desire in his detecting me, however; and I dodged his glances by turning away to ogle the contents of shop windows, slipping into shadowy alcoves, or hiding behind any nearby walls.

At the same time, I had to keep my eyes open for any suspicious characters among the similarly attired that were heading in the same direction. Even when Wilson reached Fleet Street and began to mix with the general populous, he remained in the proximity of personages from the Inns of Court. Might his pursuer be mingling unseen among them? I did identify a man of equal height and weight who was matching Wilson's pace; yet hidden as he was by bowler and scarf, I could not distinguish the stranger's features. When Wilson reached his home, however, the other man was nowhere to be seen; and to be honest, I could not swear that anyone had been trailing Wilson in the first place.

The next few days passed just as uneventfully. In spite of leaden skies and intermittent showers, Holmes and I continued our routine of watchfulness—Holmes taking the morning shifts; I, the afternoons—but no suspicious characters made themselves known.

It was late in the evening of our third day of surveillance that an irate William Wilson burst into our sitting room. I had been reading *The Times*, and Holmes had been tuning his violin.

"I hired you to watch out for my double!" Wilson shouted.

"And so we have," answered Holmes, calmly twisting a peg.

"Bah! I've seen no one."

"The way it should be," observed Holmes with a smile.

"As yet, Mr Wilson," said I, "we have been unable to corroborate your suspicions. When we have proof, you shall have it."

"Indeed," said he with an imperious look, "I *do* have it. I was visited by the man late this afternoon."

"But I saw no one following you," I protested.

"That's because he was already within my flat when I got there. No sooner did I enter than I encountered this—this—frankly—this image of myself."

"Really, Mr Wilson," said Holmes plucking at some strings. "Are we to hear of a chimera yet again?"

"I tell you, Holmes, he is *real*. He warned me to stay away from you—not to let you meddle in his relationship with me."

"And yet here you are."

"I will not be cowed, sir—not even by the threats of a phantom."

"Threats?" I questioned, raising my eyebrows. If the man had actually warned our client of harm, then the case had become more ominous.

"Yes, gentlemen, this bogey said he would kill me if I continued with my attempts to find him out. When I came here tonight, I did my best to be sure I wasn't being followed. But as you have already discovered, the creature is hard to detect."

"Did you recognise his voice?" Holmes asked.

"No. It was a hoarse whisper."

"Pity," said Holmes, picking up his bow and pointing it at Wilson. "You must be careful, Mr Wilson. Tomorrow, friend Watson and I will work in concert and lengthen our observations."

On that reassuring note, Holmes and I slipped on our coats and escorted Wilson out to the sidewalk. With a cold rain adding to the night's gloom, I secured a hansom for our caller. Only after Holmes noted no other carriages trailing the cab did he breathe a sigh of relief. There was no way to know it at the moment, of course, but that carriage ride was the last time we would see William Wilson alive.

*****

Late that same night a sharp knock rattled our door. I started at the noise, but Sherlock Holmes simply rose and went to see who it was that had come calling so late. At the threshold stood a drenched Inspector Lestrade, a look of grim determination pinching his face in spite of the rain. Holmes gestured him in; and as the policeman marched towards our fire, he held his wet bowler in one hand and passed Holmes a small white card with the other.

From what I could see, it appeared to be Holmes's visiting card containing his name, our Baker Street address, and a handwritten number. Though it could have been any one of the numerous cards Holmes distributed to his clients in identifying himself, this one was unique: tiny drops of red dappled both sides.

"Sorry to call on you so late, gentlemen," said Lestrade, "but we found your card in the pocket of a dead man, Mr Holmes. In rooms near Long Acre Street in Covent Garden."

"Good heavens, Holmes!" I exclaimed. Do you suppose—?"

"What's this?" the policeman interrupted. "Are you connected to this case? I left a corpse and a murder scene to come here. I need to find out straightaway how you are involved in this nasty business."

"To whom did I last give a card, Watson?" Holmes asked calmly. I knew he could answer the question himself, but I reckoned he was trying to slow Lestrade's pace.

"William Wilson," said I. "It was just a few days ago. You don't think—"

"*Wilson*, you say?" asked Lestrade, taking out pencil and note pad to record his findings.

"Not that I'm surprised," Sherlock Holmes muttered with a furrowed brow. "Stabbed, was he, Lestrade?"

The policeman's mouth dropped open. He often reacted in such a fashion when Holmes revealed some bit of evidence beyond the Inspector's detecting skills. "Out with it," he commanded. "Tell me what you know, or I'll be forced to think you had something to do with it yourself."

Holmes shrugged. "The man came round Monday claiming to be one William Wilson. He appeared quite the successful barrister. Chambers in Lincoln's Inn Fields."

"He also seemed quite upset," I put in.

"About what?"

Holmes sighed. "All this requires some explanation."

"I don't have time for lengthy explanations, Mr Holmes. I've just told you that I've left a corpse lying on the floor in the front room of a flat. In fact, when I found your card, I was hoping I could convince you to return with me—you and Dr Watson—to make sense of this affair. I need to get back there as quickly as I can. I have a four-wheeler outside."

Holmes shrugged again. "Care for a ride, Watson? The weather's not the best, but when Scotland Yard's finest comes a-calling, we really should not decline the invitation."

I quickly agreed, and Holmes and I donned our rain-coats and hats. We followed Lestrade out to the kerb where a growler stood waiting in the darkness. Soon we were clattering down a wet Baker Street in the direction of William Wilson's rooms.

"Watson," said Holmes, "you're the literary man. Explain to the inspector what it was that upset our caller. I find these matters regarding Poe too tedious."

"Poe?" Lestrade blinked his eyes. "You don't mean Edgar Allan Poe, the writer? The same Poe who wrote that brilliant poem, 'The Raven'?"

"The same," said I in surprise. I had never taken Lestrade for a fancier of poetry. The fact that he had heard of Poe's celebrated poem, let alone liked it, showed the vast appeal of the American's work. "There's a story by Poe called—"

Lestrade waved me off. "I'm not interested in literary theory, Doctor. Let me tell you the facts before we get there. The poor bloke arrived home and entered his rooms. At some time past eight, a grand disturbance was heard by the landlady. She ran to the victim's door, which she found ajar, and entered. After taking one look at the bloody mess, she immediately sent her boy for the local constable, who summoned help from the Yard. I arrived, surveyed the horrible scene myself, and found your card in the dead man's pocket. Which brings us up to date."

We rolled to a stop in front of Wilson's residence, an apartment block of three storeys, just as Lestrade finished his description. The two constables at the door straightened up when they saw the Inspector emerge from the carriage.

How to describe the horror we encountered inside? Chairs and end-tables were overturned; blood smears stained the walls and carpet and streaked down the window glass. Upon the floor at the centre of this gory scene lay the body of the man we knew as William Wilson. He was sprawled on his back, his right leg dangling over the edge of a small table that had been knocked on its side. Near his hand lay a large carving knife. Discarded in a corner was an open copy of a book, its pages damp with blood spots. I could see the letter from Wilson's mother spread out on the desk. It too contained spots of blood. Near us by the door, the fractured remains of a large mirror framed within a wooden hall tree stood against the wall, shards of glass shimmering on the carpet before it.

Lestrade and I remained at the door as Holmes began to scrutinise the scene. Though initially he did not approach the body, one needed no close examination of the deceased to conclude that Wilson had been attacked and that the encounter had produced this blood-soaked *abattoir*.

Holmes was generally quiet in scrutinising such scenes, but on this occasion he spoke out when he looked at the blood-spattered book. "A collection of Poe stories," he observed, "open to the last pages of 'William Wilson'." He studied the door lock, the windows, and the carpeting. He took out his glass to examine the bloodstains.

Finally, he reached the body itself, noting the cuts, the blood, the knife. Following such work, Holmes usually kept his conclusions to himself. On this night, however, he announced definitively to Lestrade, "Aside from your familiar boot marks and the man's turned-out pocket from which you obviously extracted my card, I see no evidence of another person's presence in this room."

"Surely not suicide, Holmes," said I. "Wilson didn't seem the type. Besides, no one could attack one's own person so viciously."

"We found the door ajar," the Inspector added. "The killer could have made an escape."

"Never forget, Lestrade, that every murderer leaves some trace of his presence at the scene. It is the prime tenet of detecting. As investigators, our job is to find those traces. In this room, there are none. Thus, I conclude that no one else was here besides the dead man."

Lestrade shook his head. "A murder with no murderer? This is more of that Poe business, I should judge. As much as I hate to say it, Mr Holmes, I think you must be consumed by Poe's lunatic fantasies. 'The Raven' is one thing. But it's just a poem. From what I hear, his stories are not to be believed—a murderous ape let loose in a city? A vengeful dwarf? Body parts hidden under a floor?"

"On the contrary, Lestrade," said Holmes. "It was not I, but William Wilson himself who had been consumed by Poe's stories—so much so that in his own mind, like one of

Poe's characters, he invented someone he believed was following him and whom he actually envisioned committing murder. Only it was he himself that he was really seeing, which is probably why he broke the mirror."

"Like the end of Poe's William Wilson," I said, "seeing himself in the glass."

"Exactly, Watson. That poor wretch on the floor killed himself with a long-bladed knife in the same manner as his namesake in Poe's story."

Lestrade leaned back on his heels and allowed a broad grin to work its way across his face. "It's not often I can get the best of Mr Sherlock Holmes. Yet you persist in mentioning this William Wilson. But, you see, that was *not* the dead man's name. Regardless of what he might have told you gentlemen, he was called Gordon Bleechford. His landlady gave us his lease agreement. Not only did he sign it that way, but that was how she addressed him. What's more, we knew of him at the Yard. He seems to have recently taken up cheating at cards. *Écarté* was his game. Played at the Tankerville."

Holmes allowed himself the briefest of smiles.

"William Wilson, you say?" repeated the policeman with a self-satisfied grin. "No, Mr Holmes, this time round I judge that you backed the wrong horse."

"Confound it, Lestrade!" Holmes fairly shouted. "The man's name is irrelevant. Read the letter on his desk. Learn his background. He can call himself whatever he likes. The important fact here is that no one performed this atrocious act but the victim himself."

"Unless," I felt obligated to put in, "there really *was* some sort of *Doppelgänger* that no one but Wilson could see, some spiritual double that followed him about, some villainous twin that performed this heinous act."

"Listen to yourself, Watson," said Holmes. "You're beginning to sound like Poe!"

"Some do say," Lestrade observed as he rubbed his chin, "that Edgar Allan Poe could see things in this world that others could not."

Holmes stared at the policeman in disbelief, then merely shook his head. Striding into the carpeted hallway, Holmes opened the outer door and walked down the few steps to the sidewalk and into the rain. Hailing a cab, he called to me, "Come, Watson! Back to Baker Street where reason reigns."

We left Lestrade standing in the hallway holding his bowler in one hand and scratching his head with the other.

With the horse's hooves clattering in the background, Holmes leaned over to me and said, "Let Lestrade comb the earth for a suspect. Wilson or Bleechford, whatever his name, we know what the poor man did to himself."

Of course, thought I. *What other answer can there be?*

A peal of thunder punctuated my certainty. Or mocked it.

The Adventure of the Aspen Papers

Nine-tenths of the artist's interest in [bare facts]
is that of what he shall add to them
or how he shall turn them.
--Henry James
The Art of the Novel

I

*M*rs Hudson recognised a man of noble bearing when she saw one. Those were the visitors she most often reserved for herself to introduce, leaving to the boy in livery the task of announcing the guests she deemed less important. As a consequence, when she appeared at the door of our sitting room one morning in late October of 1887, both Sherlock Holmes and I looked up with great expectation. Sensing the drama her presence created, she smoothed down her skirt, cleared her throat, and proclaimed, "Mr Henry James."

It was not that I thought she had actually recognised the cerebral American author of *Roderick Hudson* and *The Portrait of a Lady*. Rather, it was the man himself who presented quite the authoritative figure. He appeared to be in his forties, with piercing light-grey eyes, a high forehead, and thin dark hair at his ears that accented a balding pate. Combined with his short, grizzled beard and sensitive mouth, his features conveyed a sense of dignity, perspicacity, and intelligence. What is more, having recently moved to London from the States, he was attired in a smart, three-piece English suit, a gold chain stretched taut across his waistcoat. Taken as a whole, his was an image destined to command respect from anyone, even those like Mrs Hudson, who had never heard of him—let alone his reputation. Quietly, she closed the door and exited.

"Mr Sherlock Holmes?" said our visitor to my friend, somehow aware of which of us to address.

Holmes bowed slightly, introduced me, and indicated that James take a seat.

No sooner had we settled ourselves than he addressed us. "Gentlemen, I come to you—I come to you—with a problem."

Let me say from the start that for so accomplished a writer, Henry James had the startling tendency to hesitate and repeat—almost to stutter—when he spoke. And yet his manner of speech seemed less a bumbling with words, than the rehearsing of finely-tuned sentences. To spare the reader superfluous repetition, however, I have taken the liberty to minimise this characteristic throughout the narrative that follows.

In point of fact, James's voice was rich and melodious, almost mesmerizing; and I was pleased to observe that Sherlock Holmes was immediately engaged. As I have reported elsewhere, the previous spring had been a difficult time for my friend. He had been worn down by the months he had devoted to resolving the matter of the Netherland-Sumatra Company, not to mention the unpleasant business near Reigate in Surrey where ironically he had gone to regain his strength. To see him devote his complete attention to Henry James was most reassuring indeed.

I hoped it would be equally reassuring to James; for as he sat drumming his fingers on the velvet arm of the chair, he certainly looked in need of some sort of aid.

"You don't mind if I smoke," said Holmes. It was more of a statement than a question, and it left to me the obligation of offering James a cigar.

"Not today, Doctor," said he, waving off the suggestion. "I'm—I'm in need of quick answers. This is not a social call."

Holmes ignored the implied criticism with a quick smile. Filling his briar with dark shag, he asked, "How can I be of service?"

"It's a moral issue, Mr Holmes," said James and immediately got to the point. "An acquaintance of mine has gone missing. Since I'm the one responsible for having gotten him into a sticky situation, I feel responsible for finding out what's become of him." He placed one hand on top of the other, interlocking his fingers in the process. It was as if he was signalling the complexity of the story he was about to tell.

"Pray, start at the beginning," said Holmes, blowing a blue cloud upward.

"The acquaintance in question, gentlemen, one Thomas Warren, arrived in London from New York at the end of the summer. He's an aspiring young academic, though a bit headstrong and compulsive. He's a professor— an instructor—at the University of Virginia, and the two of us have exchanged some correspondence. He hopes to advance his career through a biography of the American poet, Jeremy Aspen—Jeremy Bishop Aspen."

"Jeremy Aspen," I repeated. It was a name unfamiliar to me. Holmes, who took little interest in poetry, showed no recognition at all.

Henry James pulled at his beard. He resembled a frustrated instructor, annoyed that his students had not remembered his previous lecture. "Aspen was famous for the romantic poetry he composed at the turn of the century. His devotees call him 'The Orpheus of the New World'. A few months ago, I learned through my arcane literary connections that a former paramour of Aspen, an English woman named Olivia Borden, is rumoured still to be living here in London. I forwarded this information to Professor Warren in Virginia, and so great—so intense—was his interest that he dropped everything he'd been doing and immediately sailed to England."

"Quite the dedicated scholar," I chuckled.

A frosty glare from James quieted me. "I thought so too, Doctor; but he's gone beyond so benign a description. He considers Aspen a veritable god. More to the point, he's obsessed with the idea that Miss Borden—if located—will be able to further his career. He believes that not only could she be a fountain of knowledge regarding Aspen, but that she might actually possess letters of an intimate nature from the poet himself. Such a find—such a discovery—would elevate Warren's career in an instant."

"The paramour of a poet who wrote so long ago?" said I. "She must be well advanced in years."

"Close to ninety, I should imagine," said James, waving away Holmes's smoke that had begun to envelop us all. "Her age explains Warren's haste. He rightly fears that she could die at any moment, in which case *his* opportunity would dissipate as well. Little is known of the years Aspen spent away from his home in New York, you see. Oh, we're well aware that he lived for some time in England—but nobody knows the details. The scholar—the researcher— who publishes such information would certainly receive grand honours, and now Warren—thanks in great part to my encouragement—believes he can get the answer from this old woman, a lady with whom Aspen supposedly fell in love over seventy years ago. Warren thinks this Olivia Borden must be the reclusive muse that scholars have been seeking for years."

"If these letters exist," I observed, "I imagine that in literary circles they'd be worth a fortune."

"To be sure, Dr Watson," said James. "Thomas Warren's quite right. The discovery of the letters—not to mention the woman herself—would go far to establish not only his career but also his bank account. He can't afford to miss out."

"And how well has he succeeded?" Holmes asked.

"That's just it. I don't know. Not long after he got here, he wrote me a lengthy letter. He said he'd established that the old woman really does exist and that he'd been able to track her to a run-down manor house in Southwark called The Hollows. She lives in rented rooms there with her niece."

Holmes exhaled another blue cloud. "You're a literary man, Mr James. Hasn't this singular information from Warren sparked curiosity in *you*? Why haven't you endeavoured to meet the woman yourself?"

"A fair question, Mr Holmes, but Aspen is Warren's province. He staked out the scholarly territory for himself, and I respect his boundaries. Oh, it's true that I did go there once—to The Hollows, I mean—but only after Warren had gone missing. That's when I met the niece—Rita Borden. Miss Rita, she's called, a middle-aged spinster-type, quite plain and matronly. I learned very little from her. Indeed, most all that I'm telling you I gleaned from Warren himself."

"Pah!" Holmes cried out. "Little comes from second-hand tales."

Henry James arched his eyebrows. Accomplished writer though he might be, I was certain he was unused to people discounting his narratives.

Nonetheless, he ran his hand across his balding head and continued. "Warren wrote me about an overgrown garden within the grounds. Apparently, he managed to convince the niece of his love for flora. More important, he convinced her of his need for seclusion. He told her he was a writer seeking a place to live, you see, and that he required peace and quiet in order to compose. It was the grotesqueness of just such a garden, he told her, that soothed his soul. And I should imagine that she believed him."

"Quite so," murmured Holmes, the pipe clenched firmly between his teeth.

"The niece told him that her aunt craved money; and in the end, he offered the old woman much of his life savings to rent two rooms. For a three-months' stay at The Hollows, he paid the amount he might be charged for an exclusive flat for a year—that's how important the Aspen papers are to him. Not surprisingly, the old woman agreed; and he delivered the money to her in gold in a bag of *chamois*-leather. Or so Warren told the story to me. Accompanied by his manservant, he moved in soon after and seemed to be getting along. I myself had just returned from a lengthy stay in Italy—Venice and Florence, in particular—and have been quite busy with my own writing. Quite frankly, I didn't think much about not having heard from him."

"How long has it been?" Holmes wanted to know.

Henry James looked to the ceiling the way some people do when they calculate sums. "It's three months since he moved into the house. And another few weeks since I received no answer to a letter I sent him. It was last week that I went down there—to Southwark—and encountered the niece. At first, she sounded worried. She said that she didn't know what had become of Mr Warren—that he seemed to have disappeared. And that was all. She said she didn't want to talk to me. It was quite strange, really. She seemed both reticent and direct at the same time. All around, I must tell you, The Hollows was not too inviting a place."

"And the old woman—she still lives?"

James flashed a quick smile. "Yes—as far as I know. Though I for one never got to see her."

"And the Aspen papers?" Holmes asked, taking the pipe from his mouth. "I assume that while Warren was living at The Hollows, he never stumbled across them. If he had, I suspect he would have shared that knowledge with you."

"I don't know, Mr Holmes. At the beginning of all this, I would have expected him to tell me of his discoveries. Now I'm not so sure. When I asked Miss Rita about his work, she shut the door in my face. That's when I thought of turning to you."

Sherlock Holmes put down the briar and smiled at the writer.

Good fortune was smiling upon Henry James as well. Appealing to my friend's investigative talents was a sure-fire method of engaging his services.

"I would like it very much, Mr Holmes, if you could go to Southwark—to the house—and find out what's become of Thomas Warren. It was I, after all, who set him off on this course; and it will be I who'll feel culpable should something tragic have happened to the poor fellow."

James reached into his inside coat pocket and produced a wallet.

Sherlock Holmes put up his hand to stop the writer. "Let us see what I can uncover before we talk about finances, Mr James. Perhaps there will be very little mystery at all. What say you, Watson? Are you set for an afternoon drive to Southwark in search of a missing scholar?"

I readily agreed. The page-boy could take a message to my wife, who was more than understanding when it came to matters involving Holmes. As for my surgery, I had no patients scheduled for the next day and could easily be available then if more time should be needed.

"Then it is settled. Dr Watson and I will look into this matter, Mr James. It seems quite the curious puzzle."

Shaking hands with Holmes and me, Henry James offered a formal nod. Then he turned and marched down the seventeen stairs to the outer door, his footfalls ringing steady and certain.

II

A hansom carried us to London Bridge where we crossed the river and entered the Borough of Southwark. As per James's instructions, we took the specified turnings below Long Lane and soon found ourselves in a low, wooded area where the abundance of foliage all but obliterated the afternoon sun. A final bend in the roadway brought us to the aging manor house known as The Hollows.

Owing to the massive oaks that surrounded it, the place stood draped in shadow. Two tall chimneys rose like bookends at each side of what appeared to be a single square building, its once honey-coloured walls turned black by a century of soot, grime, and neglect. The curtained windows looked dark; many on the ground floor were barred. The rusting rails of a black metal fence framed the primordial landscape, presenting to the unlucky visitor a tangle of gnarled and overgrown hedgerows.

Our driver pulled his sorrel horse up before the access road. The black metal gates, mired by the damp soil in the open-position, might gape wide for eternity.

"Do you know this place?" Holmes asked.

"Aye," said the driver, pulling down the front of his flat cap as he surveyed the gloomy scene, "but just to pass by. Nobody in there but a pair of daft old ladies. There's some what calls 'em witches, but that's just a tale. I hear they live in a couple of rooms downstairs; the rest of the place stays empty."

Holmes nodded and instructed him to wait: paying for the added time would be far easier than trying to hail another cab on this deserted road.

Amidst a dank, cloying smell that attacked our nostrils as soon as we set foot on the broken flagstones, Holmes and I carefully negotiated the irregular pathway through the unruly grounds. It came as no surprise to encounter neither bell nor knocker when we reached the entrance, and Holmes pounded on the massive oak door with his fist.

After a few moments, it was opened only a few inches by a short young woman dressed in a blouse and skirt of white linen. Through the small gap between door and wall she stared out at us suspiciously. A single eyebrow extended above both eyes, and thick black hair appeared to hang in a long plait down her back.

"*Si?*" said she in Spanish.

"Is your mistress in?" Holmes asked, but already we could sense someone approaching behind her.

"Yes?" this latter asked, stepping in front of the maid and opening the door a few inches wider. She was a heavily-built, middle-aged woman draped in a formless dress of navy blue. "Rosa doesn't speak much English. What do you want?" She wore her dark hair tightly wound in a bun, its severity accenting her prominent nose; and she stared at us with wide-set eyes. This was obviously the matronly niece, Rita Borden, about whom Henry James had spoken.

"Yes?" she asked again.

"You are Miss Borden? Miss Rita Borden?"

"I am Miss Rita. And who are you, I should like to know?"

"My name is Sherlock Homes, and we're looking for a gentleman who lodges here, Mr Thomas Warren."

"Oh," said she with a gasp "He's gone. Left suddenly. Didn't even take his man with him. It's been more than a week now—though it seems much longer . . . . "

One could hear sadness in her voice as it trailed off. But, suddenly, just as Henry James had forewarned, she countered, "And what's it to you?"

"I'm a colleague of Mr Warren," Holmes declared.

"You're another book critic then?" said she with a touch of venom.

"Not exactly. But we haven't heard from him in months, and we are concerned about his welfare."

She smirked. "He said he was interested in our garden—that's what he told my aunt. He said he wanted to rent a room, but she told him no."

"And yet," Holmes countered, "I understand that he did secure lodgings here. What changed your aunt's mind?"

"What else?" she said with a snort. "Money, of course. Lots of it. Say, you do ask a lot of questions. I don't know why I should be telling you all this."

"To help find Mr Warren, of course."

Holmes seemed to be offering hope, and she softened a bit at his response. "My aunt gets a trifling amount each year from someone in America—hardly enough for us to live on. That's why she accepted a lodger. She wants the money for *me*."

During the course of this discussion, Miss Rita had allowed the door to open wider, and it was through this larger gap that I was able to gaze upon the ancient woman herself. The maidservant had pushed a three-wheeled Bath-chair towards the door. Staring up at us from the brown, wickerwork seat was a decrepit little figure cloaked in black—or in what must have at one time been black; her dress was now a faded dark-grey, worn shiny by many years of wear. Sitting hunched over like that, she could have been a hundred years old.

Henry James's estimate, however, was probably nearer to the mark. She had to be close to ninety—infirm, frail, desiccated. Breathing seemed to be a chore as well. But it was not her cadaverous form that caused the most alarm. That distinction fell to a black veil of tightly drawn lace that covered the upper half of her visage, leaving visible only her withered lips and skeletal jaw. It was as if she were wearing a ghastly mask. Worse, in the darkness of the room, though her eyes were barely discernible, one still had the sense that they possessed the power to bore directly into one's soul.

"Who's there, Rita?" she called in a grating voice. "Who's come to disturb our afternoon?"

"Two men looking after Mr Warren." Her tone was matter-of-fact.

"Show them in, dear. *They* might have money as well."

Miss Rita led us into a large sitting room, the thick green-velvet curtains pulled shut before a row of French windows. Heavy beams ran across the ceiling, and oak panelling lined the walls. Although white sheets concealed most of the furniture, a few wooden chairs and a low mahogany table stood uncovered and ready for use in a far corner illuminated by a pair of yellow candles. One got the feeling the room had been like this for ages.

The old woman leaned forward and gestured for us to sit down in the uncovered chairs.

"We're looking for Thomas Warren, Miss Borden," Holmes said as soon as we were seated. "We know that he roomed here for months and has now disappeared. We were hoping you might shed some light on the matter."

Below the unyielding vizard, the old lady worked a small smile—more of a smirk, actually.

"He came here under false pretences," she rasped. "He said he valued our garden. He said it was exactly the sort of quiet place he was looking for in which to do his writing. He said he'd seen the garden through the fence and wanted to revive it. All it needed was some work, he said. He promised to find some geraniums or 'Jack Frost' that would flourish in the shade. He festooned the house with flowers. For weeks on end he played his game, and only lately did he show his hand."

"He talked to *me* of plants and nature as well," added Miss Rita. "At first. Then he moved on to art and books. It took him months to get round to talking about the research he did on writers. And when I asked if he knew about Jeremy Aspen, he said he didn't know the name—didn't even know Aspen was a poet, he said. The rogue was lying, of course. In point of fact, he knew lots about Aspen. But it was only early last week that he finally got round to asking about him.

106

He said that since he did research on other writers, he might as well enquire about Aspen. He wanted to know if my aunt might have some papers or letters concerning the man."

"As if I would leave Mr Aspen's papers lying about," the old lady said. In a confidential whisper she added, "Once I realised those papers were all he was interested in, I told him he would *never* get them from me." In a sudden burst of energy, she actually raised herself and hissed, "*If* I had any such papers to give, that is." This last utterance seemed to have tapped all of her strength; for after saying the words, she dropped back down in her wickered chair and appeared to fall asleep.

Miss Rita gestured sympathetically at her aunt. "It's late," said the niece, rising and moving towards the entrance hall.

When she opened the door, we could see a finger of late-afternoon sunlight poking its way through the leaves. "I fancy you won't be nosing round here again," she said, her wide eyes registering a degree of triumph as she closed the door.

"That was no great help," said I to Holmes as we walked along the broken flags. "Not only did we learn nothing about Warren, but we haven't even determined that the Aspen papers are real."

"Did you not notice, Watson, how Miss Borden spoke of the poet as '*Mr* Aspen'? When one refers to public figures that one *doesn't* know, one tends to identify them by their surnames only."

"I've never thought of the matter."

"Well, please do. We say, 'Shakespeare wrote' or 'Shakespeare said'—not *Mister* Shakespeare."

"Of course, now that you mention it."

"But when one speaks of an acquaintance, one might well employ a title like 'Mister'."

"And the old woman," I now remembered, "did indeed call the poet '*Mister* Aspen'."

"Precisely, old fellow. I'd be willing to wager that a relationship between Miss Borden and Jeremy Aspen is, as Henry James suggested, more fact that fiction."

"Then how do you explain Warren's disappearance? If she's the right lady, why would he have left?"

"Since I expect him to return, the reason doesn't concern me. No doubt, he was frustrated. He'd spent months cultivating his relationships with the two women and saw nothing come of it. As long as the papers are here, however—not to mention his manservant—he'll be back. The Aspen papers remain too important for him to abandon."

The hansom stood where we'd left it, the sorrel horse impatiently pawing the dirt.

"Back to Baker Street, if you please," Holmes instructed the driver as we climbed into the cab. To me he said, "I shall speak to the Irregulars." He was talking of the young street Arabs whom he frequently hired to provide information from the byways of London. "They can keep an eye on The Hollows for us. That way, when Thomas Warren does return, we shall know."

The carriage took off with a jolt, and Holmes leaned over to me. "After I instruct the boys, Watson, I think a dinner in the Strand might be in order."

I smiled in agreement, but Sherlock Holmes was already staring out the window submerged in thought. I do not imagine he noticed the pink and purple swirls of sunset painting the sky.

"Dead!" came the cry as the street urchin burst into our sitting room the next morning. We were just finishing breakfast when he gave us the news. "There's somebody in that house what's died! Popped their clog. Hopped the twig!"

Sherlock Holmes put down his coffee and rose to meet the lad. "Who?" he demanded.

"Dunno, do I?" said the boy, brushing a lock of dirty brown hair from his eyes. "But I seen the wagon arrive. Only there was no black feathers on the horses. And no coffin inside it. Just a bloke in a tall hat and black togs. He went into the house."

Sherlock Holmes was already donning his coat.

"Come, Watson! There's not a moment to lose! We must get to the body before it's taken away. That was the undertaker the boy saw—come to make final arrangements with Rita Borden."

*****

Thomas Warren must have been keeping his own watch on The Hollows. For no sooner had Olivia Borden died than Warren returned. In all probability, it was his manservant who had informed him of the old woman's death. In any event Warren was already there when we arrived.

Rosa admitted us, and Holmes and I introduced ourselves in the sitting room. In black suit and sombre mien, the American certainly dressed the part of a concerned mourner. Attired for a funeral, he had obviously packed his luggage for England contemplating the possibility of bereavement. Yet with those dark, penetrating eyes and black hair combed straight back, he appeared more dashing young suitor than heavy-hearted scholar.

"We're here at the behest of Henry James," Holmes told the professor. "Mr James is concerned about you and the progress of your business here."

"I'll contact him when it's appropriate," Warren said without much concern. "'*Comme il faut*', as James himself likes to say."

Holmes and I exchanged glances, but fell in line behind Warren as he crossed the sitting room and, passing through the doorway to the ground-floor sleeping quarters, led us to Olivia Borden's inner sanctum. It was there that Miss Rita stood beside the bed, the diminutive body of her aunt lying before her.

The late Olivia Borden commanded the centre of an anachronistic tableau. With her veil no longer in place, one could see the prominence of her aquiline nose and the roundness of her skull. Wrinkled hands folded on her chest, she was clothed in luminescent white, a dress no doubt kept hidden away in anticipation of this particular occasion. The threadbare quilt upon which she rested had yellowed over the years, and the bed itself might have come from another century. With small winged suns carved into a rectangular headboard the colour of dark chocolate, the entire rosewood piece suggested a Regency design. Redundant hairbrushes and depleted unguents adorned the dressing table, and a mirror replete with spidery cracks presided over the futile *homage* to vanity. Atop the nearby chest of drawers, a japanned wooden box that could have contained any number of rings or necklaces or letters stood conveniently open— open and empty. Owing to the dusty white drapes that covered the windows, the whole scene, illuminated as it was by floor-candelabras on either side of the bed, seemed a setting from some antique mystery play.

Warren had positioned himself next to Miss Rita and bowed his head. Despite his show of sympathy, I felt certain that his concern dealt less with the dead woman than with the papers he had suspected her of possessing, the same papers—if they existed at all—presumably now in the custody of her niece.

We took our cue from Miss Rita and, following a decent period of respect, prepared to exit. I made one last visual sweep of the chamber, hoping to detect the evidence of someone's final frantic search for the missing papers. But aside from the open wooden box, there appeared no signs of any such disruption.

As I turned to leave, however, Holmes caught my arm. "Watson," he whispered. "Engage the others in conversation elsewhere. I need time to examine this room more fully."

"I wonder," he now said to Miss Rita, "if you'd mind giving me a moment alone with your aunt. Many people will tell you that I am a private person who prefers to keep his personal thoughts strictly between the deceased and himself."

"You hardly knew the woman," she scoffed, but Holmes seemed sincere; and fortunately Miss Rita, no great master of recognizing deceit, did not require further convincing. For his part, Warren seemed eager to talk. Indeed, no sooner did we find our places in the sitting room than he began discussing what he knew of the elder Miss Borden and Jeremy Aspen.

"Looking at that old woman," said he, "you wouldn't think her to have been a beautiful, vivacious, even rebellious young lady. But she must have been *all* those things. It would explain why Aspen was so attracted to her. For that matter, I often wonder how they met."

Miss Rita shrugged. "He came calling on her."

"I know *that*," replied the professor, "but why? Aspen was an aristocrat; Miss Borden's background was more modest. What prompted him? My own guess is that she must have been connected to someone with whom the poet had dealings here in England. She could have been a governess to a child of one of Aspen's friends. Or the daughter of someone he'd employed—a secretary, perhaps, or a portrait painter. Americans love to have their images immortalised by English artists. Whatever the circumstances, she held the man's attention—so much so that she became the object of his love. She was, after all, the precious *'l'ange'* in his cycle of love sonnets."

I shrugged my shoulders, hoping that the conversation would prevent the others from wondering what Holmes was up to.

Suddenly, Warren's eyes flashed, and he changed the subject. "I think she hid his letters somewhere." He pointed at a tall mahogany secretary's desk with brass fittings. "That was my first choice. I'd always suspected it was locked, but I couldn't be sure. Yet I was afraid to look. Not that I would ever steal the papers, mind you; but a few weeks before her death, I finally worked up the courage to see if the desk would open. I was just about to test the lock when the old lady interrupted me."

"Why," Rita cried, "that must have been just before you left."

"In truth," Warren said, "with that black veil of hers, she gave me quite the fright. 'Stop that!' she'd cried out while teetering on her cane in the doorway—all those months and I didn't even know she could walk. In such a fury was she that she tore off that infernal mask and threw it to the floor. That was when I saw her magnificent eyes."

"My word," I barely whispered.

"Oh, yes—her eyes. They were wide and deep and full of hatred. And yet, strange to say, they also filled me with a kind of comfort. For looking into those extraordinary orbs, I somehow felt closer to Aspen. Her rage at me was a short-lived imitation of the torrid flames that must have burned so brightly when she was in his arms, a fiery passion that I thought had been all but extinguished."

Warren's own eyes were wide open now, a man staring full-on into a vibrant past as he described the confrontation.

"'I know what you're looking for,' the old woman screeched at me, '—why you've come here.' She nodded at the secretary desk. "Go ahead and look inside, if you must.' Reluctantly, I tried the lid and, discovering that it was unlocked after all, lifted it open. I expected to discover nothing, and nothing is precisely what I found. The old woman stared triumphantly at me.

"It was when she turned and hobbled resolutely back to her room that I realised she would never be giving me the letters. Mortified—and not a little angry at Olivia Borden—I left the house the next day."

Miss Rita sat open-mouthed. There was obviously a lot about her aunt she had apparently never got to know.

Just then Rosa entered the room with two large vases of Calla lilies.

"I ordered them," Warren said.

A look of admiration appeared in Miss Rita's wide-set eyes. I couldn't say whether she had ever experienced a social engagement with a man, but she was certainly appreciative of Warren's gesture.

I, on the other hand, was more cynical. With the papers as Warren's goal, I could not help regarding all of his acts as empty motions designed to get Miss Rita to share her aunt's literary trove with him. In fact, I was beginning to suspect that the letters had motivated the behaviours of everyone in that house. Why, perhaps the old woman had been dangling them in front of the professor to unite him with her niece. Or perhaps the middle-aged spinster herself was hoping to inherit them and use them to entice the man.

Holmes's return interrupted my thoughts. He arrived in the sitting room just as Miss Rita was rising to help Rosa set up the flowers.

"It's a bit stuffy in here," he observed, striding to the green-velvet drapes. Drawing one of them aside, he opened the French window an inch or two. As he moved the curtain back in position, he turned back to Miss Rita. "One last question, if I may. Did your aunt write a will?"

Miss Rita looked down. "No. She had nothing to leave me."

"Except for the papers," Thomas Warren muttered.

Holmes glared at the professor, but all he said to him was, "Don't fail to let Henry James know that you're safe." Then he motioned to me that it was time to leave, and once more we expressed our condolences to Miss Rita.

"If you don't mind my asking," Holmes said to her, as we were about to exit, "should I want to pay my respects yet again, when will the undertaker come for your aunt."

"At nine o'clock tomorrow morning."

With Holmes nodding at the information, we left that frightful house and hurried back to our waiting hansom. I climbed in as under darkening skies my friend exchanged a few words with the driver. Then Holmes joined me, and we began our journey back to Baker Street. Or so I thought.

IV

After making the first turn that hid us from The Hollows, the cab came to an abrupt halt. The horse whinnied in protest, but Holmes stepped out and bade me follow. As I would learn later, he had arranged earlier for the driver to stop once the house was out of sight, and Holmes dropped a healthy number of compensatory coins into the man's hand. As the hansom disappeared in the darkness, the two of us stood out in the road listening to the diminishing clink of the horse's hooves.

"Should anyone be watching," he explained, "I wanted it to appear that we'd actually left. The old woman was murdered, Watson; and I fear there may be more violence yet to come."

"Murdered?" I cried. "But she looked so peaceful, Holmes. What makes you say such a thing?

"You know my methods, old fellow. As soon as I was alone with the body, I drew my lens and examined the corpse. It was absurdly simple to discover the bits of down in Miss Borden's nostrils, the tiny feathers she must have inhaled gasping for her final breaths with a pillow held down over her face."

"Who could have committed so heinous an act?"

"That is what I hope to confirm tonight."

"But, Holmes, surely we must inform the police."

"We don't have the time," said he, shaking his head. He then motioned me to follow, continuing his explanation as we edged back down the dark road towards The Hollows. "We know that Olivia Borden's body will be collected by the undertaker tomorrow morning at nine. I fear that the immediacy of that appointment may precipitate some harmful action."

"You think that Miss Rita is in danger then?"

Holmes smiled. "On one level, I think not. The death of the old woman leaves the niece as the sole link to the papers. Anyone seeking the papers would be foolish to silence her."

"Unless," I added, "the miscreant has already acquired them."

"If he had acquired them, Watson, he would no longer be here." We were approaching the house now, and Holmes lowered his voice. "When I searched the old woman's room, I spied a blanket and sheet that appeared dishevelled on the far side of the bed. I immediately ran my hand beneath the upper mattress."

"Did you find anything?"

"A single scrap of very old foolscap containing a few strokes of faded ink. But even so small a morsel was enough to suggest that somehow the withered old woman had mustered the strength to hide the papers between her mattresses."

"Surely such a hiding place could not be secure. When Rosa changed the bedding, she'd discover the cache."

"You're right, of course," replied Holmes. "Perhaps Olivia Borden had originally kept them in the secretary desk just as Warren suspected or even in the japanned box so conveniently left open for us. But move them she did, and somehow—maybe with Rosa's help—hid them beneath her mattress. In any case, I suspect that Rita has found her aunt's hiding place—or may even have been given the papers. At the very least, Rita is probably the only one who knows their current location."

I was about to respond; but we had reached the railing of the metal fence, and Holmes put his finger to his lips. In the darkness, we slipped through the open gates and tiptoed to the garden at the side of the building. It was here that we encountered the French window that Holmes had earlier so presciently left open. Although we could see nothing of the sitting room through the curtained glass, we could hear quite clearly the conversation that was going on inside.

"I thought that you *liked* spending time with me," Miss Rita was saying to Warren.

"Of course, I do," said the professor. "I enjoy your company. Remember those summer evenings out in the garden?"

"Yes," she sighed. "They were grand." One could hear the longing in her voice. "For years I've been imprisoned here with my aunt. And then *you* came round, someone who took an interest in me."

There was a moment of awkward silence. I imagined Warren dwelling on her final few words. "Now listen," he said at last. "I don't believe I've ever acted in an ungentlemanly manner towards you."

"I thought that the flowers—"

"They were intended for your aunt as well as for you."

"So *you* might get the papers. Perhaps that's what my aunt was thinking all along. In the end, bringing you and me together must have meant more to her than spending her final hours with her niece."

But Warren would not continue Miss Rita's narrative. "I should imagine that all along her plan had been to give me the papers."

"No!" said Miss Rita firmly. "She never wanted outsiders to get their hands on them." There was a pause of a few moments during which Miss Rita must have been fashioning her most convincing smile and most flirtatious voice. "Now if you were a *relation* . . ."

The word could have but one meaning.

"Me—and *you*?" Warren spat out.

"I've enjoyed our time together."

"But for the rest of our lives?" One could not ignore the disdain in his voice. "Not even the receipt of *all* your aunt's papers would be worth such misery!"

We heard her gasp and then the rustle of clothing and the stomp of heavy feet. Warren had obviously stood and was about to make a grand exit up the stairs to his room. "I'll be leaving in the morning!" he shouted. "Early!"

Muted sobs filled the silence.

*****

Sitting cross-legged on the damp ground by the open window, Holmes and I managed to stay awake through an uneventful night. With only the routine activities of nocturnal creatures to distract us—mice scrabbling among the tree roots, crickets drumming their songs, an owl hooting his displeasure at our presence—we had to wait until the next morning for human passions to become enflamed.

Sometime before dawn, Holmes reached inside the window, which no one had bothered to close, and adjusting the green-velvet curtains that had blocked our view, created a gap of about half-an-inch through which we could peer. The morning activities in the house played out before us as if we were attending the theatre. Off-stage, the clatter of dishes and clanging of pans announced that Rosa was preparing breakfast in the kitchen. At half-seven, Miss Rita made her entrance from the sleeping quarters on the ground floor. Dressed in austere black, she was prepared for her meeting

118

with the undertaker. At almost the same moment, as if he had been waiting for Miss Rita to appear, Thomas Warren emerged from his chamber and hurried down the stairs. Despite his threat to leave before the removal of the body, he wore the same black suit we'd seen the previous day. Miss Rita turned at his approach, a melancholy look colouring her downcast face.

"I'm sorry," Warren said, reaching for her right hand. "I've been cruel. I should have taken your proposal more seriously last night."

She raised her head.

"In fact," he said, sounding full of contrition, "I've given myself the chance to examine your offer once more, and I believe I now see much wisdom in its implementation. I owe my career to the securing of those papers; and while I did all I could in the most proper way to obtain them from your aunt, I believe she never seriously appreciated my efforts. I think that for as long as she lived, she intended to use those papers as bait to bring me closer to you."

Miss Rita's wide eyes looked even wider. And more melancholy. Perhaps she sensed what Warren was about to suggest.

"In fact, I now believe that we should honour your aunt's wishes and agree to such a union. I believe she intended for you to do with the papers exactly as you had proposed to me last night. I am, you see, quite prepared to accept your aunt's papers—the Aspen papers, if you will—as a dowry."

At some point during Warren's last few words, Miss Rita's left hand had begun a slow journey upward until it was covering her now open mouth.

"Why, what's the matter?" asked Warren. "I know it's what you want. Everyone will be pleased. You will get a husband; I will get the letters; and your aunt's memory will be honoured."

Miss Rita lowered her head.

"What's the matter?" Warren asked again. His eyes signalled fear; his tone had grown desperate.

"Oh, Thomas," she said slowly, "I burned the papers last night. In the fireplace in my bedroom. Once you refused me, I saw no point in keeping them."

"You—you *burned* them? The key to my life's work?"

"I was going to have them buried with my aunt," she explained, realizing that she'd also destroyed any future she might have envisioned with this man. "But you made me so angry last night that I burned them one by one. It took a long time."

Warren's eyes began to bulge. "After what I've already done?" he muttered, his face turning dangerously red.

"What?"

"And to think," he snarled, "I almost found you charming."

"We can still marry," Miss Rita urged. "You'll see. I can make you a good wife."

Thomas Warren glared at her. The silence seemed interminable. In the end, he threw back his head and laughed. It began as a loud, raucous laugh, but it slowly transformed itself into a maniacal shriek. Suddenly, he was upon her, his white fingers tightly gripping her throat.

Without a word, Holmes sprang up, jerked open the French window and raced towards the struggling pair. Wrapping an arm around Warren's neck, he yanked him off the poor woman, who fell heavily to her knees on the hardwood floor.

In an instant, I had joined Holmes; and between us we managed to wrestle Thomas Warren onto one of the sheet-covered chairs. Rosa ran out from the kitchen to see what the trouble was. She helped her mistress to stand, and Holmes ordered her to go out in the street to find the nearest constable.

"*La policía!*" he instructed.

Soon we heard the blast of a police whistle, and within the hour Inspector Gregson arrived at The Hollows.

Not long thereafter, we had the satisfaction of seeing Thomas Warren charged with the murder of Miss Olivia Borden—whom he confessed to smothering after he had secretly returned to the house—and the attempted murder of Miss Rita Borden. Between two uniformed officers, he was marched to the police van, which immediately drove off in the direction of Scotland Yard.

As it clattered down the road, it passed the undertaker's hearse, which was just then approaching the house from the opposite direction.

V

The next afternoon, Henry James joined us for tea at Baker Street. Following Warren's arrest, Holmes had sent a request to the writer at his rooms in De Vere Gardens, and James eagerly accepted. In addition to the tea, Mrs Hudson set out small chocolate biscuits and a few of the sugary doughnuts that, according to Holmes, James was known to enjoy.

Sherlock Holmes reported the details of the case to our guest as we sampled our tea.

"Good Lord," said James, when Holmes had finished. "I had no idea my letter regarding Jeremy Aspen would create—would weave—such a tangled skein."

"More tangled than you can imagine, Mr James," Holmes observed. "For it is my conjecture that the Aspen papers contained more value of a personal nature than even your world of *belles-lettres* could estimate. I have no valid proof, you understand; but judging from my own observations—the similar facial structures, the widespread eyes, the curved nose—not to mention the concern that Olivia Borden expressed regarding her niece's welfare—I can only conclude that a major topic of the correspondence between Jeremy Aspen and his mistress was the welfare of their child—a daughter I believe to be Miss Rita Borden."

At this revelation, the doughnut Henry James was poised to devour fell onto his plate.

I found myself equally astonished. After catching my breath, I asked Holmes, "And does Miss Rita know of your conjecture?"

"Only if she read the letters before she burned them—and, of course, only if my supposition is accurate. Based on so little evidence, it is certainly nothing I would share with her."

James retrieved his doughnut and took a small bite and then another. "So," he said after finishing the morsel, "in addition to the tale—the mystery—surrounding the Aspen papers, we also have a story dealing with the secret love-child of a writer and his mistress. Not to mention the cunning machinations of a so-called scholar."

"Just so, Mr James," said Holmes.

The author did not respond for a moment. Staring off as they were, his grey eyes suggested his mind was somewhere else. If my own writing experiences might serve as a guide, I imagined him already at work, composing in his head some sort of novel dealing with the bizarre triangle of old woman, forlorn niece, and obsessed academic.

"One writer to another, Mr James," I dared to say, "quite a story, is it not?"

"Indeed, Dr Watson. Perhaps one we might both attempt to record—each in his own fashion, of course."

"An excellent suggestion," said I, already devaluing my factual narrative when compared with the intimate psychological embellishments so typical of James's fiction. His ornate and methodical style could perfectly reflect the labyrinthine twists and turns of a mind diseased.

"I would, of course, purge the story of obvious references," said he. "I could fudge or doctor my notebooks—change Jeremy Aspen to Byron. Or Shelley. And shift the scene of the adventure to somewhere outside of London. Maybe even outside of England." Suddenly, he clapped his hands together, the notion of subterfuge obviously gaining in appeal. "This very afternoon I shall walk—no, I shall drive—to the National Gallery and look at landscapes for inspiration. Turner's watercolours of Venice might be just the thing!"

Sherlock Holmes poured himself more tea. "I envy you, Mr James. The world of detection offers no such escape. *My* boundaries are limited by the rules of logic and the confines of reality. The detective cannot go willy-nilly where inspiration calls him."

"Ah, yes, Mr Holmes," said Henry James. "But it is the claustrophobia created by such rules that leads the literary artist to the world of fiction. Imagination trumps reality every time."

Such abstract arguments usually make my head spin. But on this occasion, I was ready to do battle. "I—I take your remark about writing a story as a challenge, sir," said I to Henry James. "Let us each report the sordid tale of the Aspen papers in our own manner and leave it to posterity to judge who has rendered the stronger case."

With a smile, Holmes pointed first at the gasogene and then at the spirit case. I understood his gestures and, producing three glasses, mixed the sparkling water with brandy. Once everyone was served, we hoisted our drinks.

"To the judgment of posterity," proclaimed Sherlock Holmes.

"Hear, hear," Henry James chimed in, and then the three of us emptied our glasses.

For Want of a Sword

I

*A*lthough *the gathering marked a ten-year-anniversary, it was not a celebration in the usual sense, but more of a memorial. I had no prior knowledge of the occasion save for the small white card I had received earlier in the day from Mr Sherlock Holmes. Billy the page hand-delivered the message, which was dated 22nd June 1903 and read:*

My dear Watson,
Join Mycroft and me at the Diogenes Club this evening at 8.00. New material to add to your histories. Wear mourning black.

More of a command than an invitation, it was signed with the single letter "S".

I have written elsewhere that no matter how demanding, it has always been difficult for me to refuse any requests from Sherlock Holmes. They always present so many intriguing possibilities, and tonight's appeared no different.

"Of course, you should go, John," said my wife, a most understanding woman when it came to my friendship with Holmes. "And please offer my condolences for whoever it is who has died."

"I wish I knew," I answered.

Whoever indeed? *I found myself pondering that question throughout our dinner of lamb and potatoes. Curiosity prompting, I hurried through the orange sorbet, more than ready to don black suit and cravat*

"How do I look?" *I asked my wife once I had dressed.*

"Suitably funereal," *she replied with a half-smile, still struck, no doubt, by the selfsame mix of interest and sympathy that were continuing to plague me. Assuring her I would provide a complete report upon my return, I secured a black band on my trilby and hailed a hansom.*

It was a beautiful evening for a drive. In what had been a very wet June, temperatures were finally on the rise; and the seemingly constant blanket of clouds had all but dissipated. As we clattered along beneath the darkening sky, a few stars were beginning to twinkle and the lights of the city to take hold. On so splendid an evening, not even the thought of being cooped up in Mycroft's stodgy club could dampen my spirit—especially when charged with the question of who it might be that the brothers Holmes were remembering.

I alighted directly in front of the Diogenes in the western end of Pall Mall, the home of so many of London's distinctive and celebrated clubs. Maypoole, the ancient doorman, took my hat and bade me enter. Though it felt as if my arrival had been expected, the man offered no hint concerning the nature of the event I was there to attend.

Certainly, *I thought as I tiptoed up the stairs to the Strangers' Room,* there are no clues to be gained from Holmes's recent activities. *Earlier in the month he had solved the riddle of the Mazarin Stone; but as far as I knew, he had no new cases with which to occupy himself. Oh, there had been a time when Sherlock Holmes would have raged* against such inactivity; but by the summer of '02 it was common knowledge to those with whom he was acquainted that he was planning to retire soon and that, as a consequence, he remained uninterested in acquiring additional clients.

"Ah, Watson," said Holmes as I silently entered the Strangers' Room, "so good of you to join us."

Behind me, a serving man in a white tunic glided silently out the door. He had just finished placing a cut-glass bowl filled with almonds and Brazil nuts on the low mahogany table. A decanter of similar cut-glass design had already supplied two small copitas with a ruby-red port. A third glass, presumably mine, remained empty.

Dressed in traditional mourning attire, the two Holmes brothers rose to greet me—my friend easily enough, Mycroft with a great deal of difficulty punctuated with an elongated grunt. On account of the lingering twilight that dimly illuminated the large bow window, they appeared before me in silhouette, their figures accounting for the difference in their efforts. Sherlock Holmes stood tall and thin. His brother, though of similar height, carried much greater weight. Despite the celebrated acuity of Mycroft's mind, the least physical movement seemed to him an anathema.

We shook hands all round and exchanged warm greetings, not a common experience in the Diogenes Club. As faithful readers will remember, the establishment, founded by a group of men that included Mycroft himself, was desirous of strict quietude and thus maintained a list of rules that forbade all nature of speech within the walls. Only here in the Strangers' Room, a venue set aside for just such occasions as tonight's, would speech be tolerated.

"Gentlemen," said I, taking the leather armchair indicated by Mycroft, "I am pleased to be here though I must confess that ever since I received the invitation, I've been wondering for just whom this memorial has been planned."

The brothers exchanged well-practiced glances; and once they too had seated themselves, Mycroft nodded at his younger brother.

Sherlock Holmes filled the empty glass before me with port and then refilled Mycroft's as well as his own. Handing one glass to his brother and another to me, he stood again and indicated that we should join him. Once more, Mycroft struggled to his feet; and when we were all three facing one another, Holmes raised his glass.

"To Admiral George Tryon and the three–hundred–fifty-eight brave lives lost," he proclaimed with due solemnity, "in the sinking of H.M.S. Victoria *on this same date ten years ago—22 June 1893."*

Of course.

We drank and remembered.

Though I had not that day recalled the anniversary to which Holmes had alluded, no true Englishman could ever forget the catastrophe. During military manoeuvres in the Mediterranean a decade before, two British warships, the Victoria *and the* Camperdown, *had tragically collided. By all accounts, the results were devastating. The* Victoria, *pierced below the waterline some nine feet by the steel battering ram of the* Camperdown, *required less than fifteen minutes to sink. As evidenced in Holmes's toast, the resultant loss of life was immense. There were those within the Admiralty who labelled it the most disastrous accident in the history of the Royal Navy.*

The sheer horror of the tragedy was quite sufficient to make it memorable, but the event maintained a personal connection to Sherlock Holmes and me as well. The collision had occurred off the coast of Syria at the same time that Holmes—presumed dead following his encounter with Professor Moriarty at the Reichenbach Falls—happened to be travelling incognito through the Levant. Upon that day in particular, he found himself in Tripoli, a part of Syria before the Great War, where he actually witnessed the horrible accident first-hand.

As it turned out, the British press was either too reluctant or simply forbidden to print anything critical about the much-loved Royal Navy. But through a series of complicated events, some of which I would later chronicle in the account I titled The Seventh Bullet, *Holmes managed to convey the story by telegraph to the American pressman, David Graham Phillips, the newly appointed London correspondent for Joseph Pulitzer's newspaper,* The World. *As a result, despite Pulitzer's reluctance to publicise his pressmen's by-lines, Phillips gained international fame for reporting the story. To thank Holmes for his help in sending out the details, the dapper Phillips had actually come to visit us at Baker Street in 1896. Sad to say, it was this same friendship that would ultimately lead us to New York years later to investigate the writer's untimely murder. That enquiry, of course, was still years off and another matter entirely.*

I assumed it was the Graham-Phillips aspect of the disaster that had sparked Holmes's desire to remember the lost seamen. As for Mycroft, I could not account for his lingering sentimentality unless it was due to his relationship, however opaque, with the Foreign Office and the Ministry of Defence.

No matter the reason, paying our respect to the naval dead was an honourable gesture. Yet once having done so, I felt it equally appropriate to honour our friend Phillips. It was he, after all, who had brought the matter to the public's attention. Raising my glass a second time, I offered, "To Graham Phillips and the printed word."

"Graham Phillips," Holmes echoed with a smile and proceeded to drink.

Mycroft, however, furrowed his massive brow and resumed his seat. "I salute the dead of the Victoria,*" said he tartly, "not the conniving Yank who almost single-handedly set back the forces of peace in Europe."*

"Now, now, Mycroft," said my friend as he and I also settled back in our chairs. "I believe you're overstating the case."

"Am I?" replied Mycroft, leaning forward with some effort to grab a handful of nuts. "Of course, I'd expect you to say that, Sherlock. To admit otherwise is to confess your own sorry role in the delicate affair—not to mention your Bohemian naiveté. *There was much going on behind the scenes, brother-mine, of which you had not an inkling." He placed an almond in his mouth and emphasised his accusation with a definitive chomp.*

I looked from one Holmes to the other, each with clenched jaw and fixed gaze. It was clear that though ten years might have passed, the tension over the matter had not.

Sherlock Holmes suddenly focused his gaze on me. *"I say," he suggested to Mycroft, "why not let Watson here be the judge? As much as it will pain me to recount the horrors of that day, I shall detail for him my recollection of the events, and you may offer him yours. I'm sure that with the passage of an entire decade, your secrets can safely be exposed."*

Mycroft knitted his brows again as he considered the offer. Finally, he nodded. "As long as you understand that some constraints still bind me," he cautioned, "I'll drink to that proposal." Without rising this time, he drained the rest of the ruby liquid from his copita and popped another almond into his mouth.

Sherlock Holmes moved to refill our drinks, and I offered him my glass. At the same time, I could not help noting that no one had asked for my own opinion about participating in such a debate. I should laugh. With the steel-grey eyes of both Holmes brothers trained upon me, I knew it would be virtually impossible to deny their collective will. Besides, though I already possessed some familiarity with the grim outline of Holmes's narrative, I confess to anticipating with great interest any new secrets of state that Mycroft Holmes might volunteer to divulge.

What follow are the respective statements of both brothers.

II

Sherlock Holmes's Account

How I came to be in Syria following my flight from the falls of Reichenbach remains a tale for another time. Suffice it to say that the ancient mysteries of the Arab world have always beckoned; and following some two years spent in Tibet, I made my way to the Middle East. By the early summer of '93, bearing a rucksack and draped in white *kafeyah* and loosely-woven *haik*, I had traversed a good part of Persia and, civil unrest notwithstanding, gone on to investigate the treasures of Mecca. Then—who knows, Watson, perhaps inspired by your old portrait of the murdered General Gordon—I put aside my knowledge of all the blood spilt in Khartoum and decided to travel to that historic city as well.

I knew that ports in the Levant offered a wide array of ships bound for northern Africa, and so I set out from Mecca for the west coast of Syria. In spite of some harrowing adventures along the way, I eventually found myself in a wagon laden with wool prayer rugs lumbering through the Syrian highlands northeast of Tripoli.

The driver, a grizzled old man with deep-set eyes, took me along the twisting paths through the mountains, but it wasn't until mid-day of 22nd June that I actually observed the seaport. In point of fact, the old man had purposely pulled up his horse when we reached a broad turning in the road. He had wanted to give me the proper vantage for my first look at the glorious panorama below—the small white houses sprinkled about the descending foothills, the ebony cluster of ships' masts bobbing by the wooden docks, and the vast, deep-blue Mediterranean whose gentle waves shimmered brightly beneath the overhead sun. I tell you, gentlemen, it was a sight to behold; but like its more celebrated Edenic counterpart, this paradise too contained its dangers—in particular, a tell-tale blot of dark smoke off in the distance serving to mar the scene.

The old man followed my gaze. He spoke little English, but none the less pronounced the familiar word, "Bri-tish."

Extracting the field glasses from my rucksack for a better look, I immediately saw that he was correct. Far to the south—splayed out for two miles, single-line abreast—sailed eleven warships, each flying the Union Jack.

"British," I repeated with a nod.

Indeed, there could be no doubt that this was Her Majesty's grand Mediterranean Fleet. Through the glasses, I could clearly see the large flagship and her pair of massive guns mounted low in a single turret at the prow. She was accompanied by a line of other low-slung, ironclad steamers—by my reckoning, eight battleships and three large cruisers in all.

It was quite a display. Oh, they may have lacked the billowing white sails of the splendid vessels from yesteryear, but I knew that those ships before me featured the strongest and most modern weapons in the world. The Mediterranean provides England a gateway to the East—to the Ottoman Empire, the Suez Canal, and ultimately India. The Royal Navy is not about to let so important a shipping lane be interrupted by any foreign nation dim enough to have forgot that Britannia rules the waves.

I lowered the glasses so I could watch the entire Fleet approach the wide waters of the bay in which they would ultimately be anchoring. The vessels themselves may have appeared small in the vastness of the scene, but one couldn't miss the cloud of black smoke that had originally caught my attention. Rudely belched from the steamers' funnels, it was now spreading throughout the calm sea air. Beneath this ominous veil, the ships seemed to travel in a kind of darkness, the cloud itself dissipating into purposeless wisps only after drifting far astern.

It was a warm summer's day—nearly eighty degrees, I should judge—and the humidity was already causing the air to feel close. In short, conditions augured just the sort of afternoon any sensible Englishman would choose to remain indoors. And yet with the prospects of a grand naval spectacle about to unfold before me, I nodded to my driver to proceed down the dusty road to the sea so I could have a closer look. Hours later, he deposited me near the wharves where, after offering thanks for his services, I paid him what he asked and then some. The piping of sea birds announced my arrival.

Before approaching the water, however, I realised I had business to conduct. Ever since the wagon had rattled past the central telegraph office in the heart of Tripoli, I had been thinking of sending a cable to Mycroft. He and I had been out of communication for the last few weeks; and now that I had reached a seaport on my journey to Khartoum, I thought it time not only to inform him of my whereabouts, but also to ask him for additional funds.

(What, Watson, still the long face after all these years? You know I couldn't contact *you*. Recall that during my travels, I needed to keep my existence unknown from the remnants of Moriarty's gang. I couldn't risk your open and honest nature revealing my secret, old fellow. Mycroft remained my only confidant; and even when communicating with him, I identified myself as the Norwegian explorer, "Sigerson".)

Upon nearing the docks, I spied an old woman selling *hummus* and flat bread. Hungry as I was and in need of information, I purchased her wares and, using my hands to imitate the action of writing, made her understand that I was seeking a telegraph office. She pointed down the road and with the wave of her fingers indicated a pair of turns. I thanked the woman, followed her rudimentary instructions, and soon found myself standing before a small, whitewashed building not more than a mile distant from the sea.

A few steps took me inside where I saw a squat, bearded man perched behind a barren desk. It took but a moment to ascertain that he knew no English, only French and Arabic. But after I printed out a brief note and offered him some money, he dispatched my cable with little problem. Munching on a piece of the flat bread I'd stored in my rucksack, I exited the telegraph office; and along alleyways crowded with weathered sailors, wide-eyed travellers, and shrewd buyers and sellers of anything one could imagine, I made my way to the docks.

The salty smell of the sea embraced me as I edged past busy fish stalls, piles of sails, and rows of wooden boats. I removed my boots upon reaching the strand and ambled through the pebbles at the water's edge. By 3.30 I found a deserted stretch of sand along the bay's eastern shore—not far, as it so happened, from the stone ruins of the Tower of Lions, an ancient, square-sided fortress adorned with worn-down carvings of the king of beasts. Unknown to me at the time, it was to serve as a landmark for the British Fleet.

The sun was now baking hot. The warships, still a few miles out, were pointed in my direction—that is, towards the eastern edge of the bay. From where I was positioned, I could easily discern their white upper works, long black hulls, and polished brass fittings. With the thrumming of the steam engines as background, I squatted on the beach to watch the show.

Whatever my notable talents, gentlemen, knowledge of naval manoeuvres is not among them. At first, I was content to gawp at the military splendour of the vessels—the colourful flags, the disciplined formation, the mighty guns. I confess to you that it was truly quite sufficient for stirring one's national passions, especially those of the traveller so many miles from home. Yet within a few short minutes even I could see cause for concern.

In order to enter the bay, the broad line of ships had magically rearranged itself into a pair of close, parallel files. The two divisions were just now heading into port, and anyone with a cursory knowledge of measurements could intuit that, as they neared the shore, they would by necessity very soon—that is to say, almost immediately—have to turn about or risk running into the boats already at anchor—if not into the very docks themselves. The closer they sailed, the more distressed I became, unable to comprehend their failure to reverse direction.

Within seconds, however, all seemed to be righted. The flagship began her turn, and I breathed a sigh of relief. Obviously, or so I assumed, *all* the ships in both columns would turn-about in the same manner at the same time and continue sailing in reverse order in the direction from which they had come. Such a course seemed the reasonable manoeuvre. Yet moments later the lead ship of the second file also began to turn—but to turn *inward, towards* the flagship! There could not have been more than a thousand yards between them—surely not enough space for the two lines to turn safely *towards* each other, one after another. And yet that was precisely what they seemed bent on doing!

Alas, there was no time to ponder the options. The two lead ships—the *Victoria* and the *Camperdown,* I was soon to learn—were turning directly into each other. Within seconds and at an almost perfect right angle, the *Camperdown* ploughed straight into the *Victoria.*

Gentlemen, I tell you, it was an event that I shall never forget! Everyone watching—on the hills, on the strand, on the docks—heard the impact, an explosive roar that ripped through the clouds of dust and dirt filling the air, a cacophony of noise trailing in its wake: the screams of frightened bluejackets, the trill of a bugler's call to action, and finally the mournful lament of the *Camperdown's* foghorn.

I sprang to my feet at the initial contact, grabbing my binoculars and shielding the sun from my eyes. There was nothing I could do, of course, save stand and observe—though I did check my watch. It was 3.34.

A shudder surged through me as with an ear-splitting, half-human shriek, the *Camperdown* now slowly backed away, its engine thrown into reverse and the underwater ram—about which I would only hear later—surgically extracting itself from its victim. By 3.36 the ships had separated, but the *Victoria's* low-slung prow was already dipping dangerously low. It had taken only two minutes to complete the act; and yet the damage was not unlike Hamlet's prick of Laertes: "a hit—a very palpable hit."

The scene came alive with confusion. Lifeboats dropped from the nearby ships even as those large vessels were manoeuvring out of the way of the two damaged craft. And all the while, the *Victoria* continued to take on water. In only five minutes, her bows had sunk some fifteen feet, and the sea was beginning to lap at the muzzles of her huge guns. A few minutes later, with a sickening rip, the gun-turret broke free; and as the pair of long barrels slid forward over the deck, their weight lowered the prow ever farther until the stern of the ship began to rise out of the water. Through my field glasses, I could actually see her turning screws break the white surface of the now-roiling sea.

At the same time, displaying unimaginable discipline, some six hundred of the *Victoria's* bluejackets lined up four-deep on the deck to await instructions. In point of fact, they were anticipating the command to leap into the ocean. Suddenly, the ship lurched to her starboard side, and even I could hear the cry of "Jump! Jump!" from an officer on the deck.

The *Victoria* was capsizing! And hundreds of bluejackets—swimmers and non-swimmers alike—dived into the water to escape being dragged down. At 3.43—a mere nine minutes after the collision—the ship rolled over and, keel up, began to spin full-circle like the needle of a compass—slowly at first, but quickly gaining speed.

Now, with water pouring into the furnaces, an explosion blasted from below. The boilers had burst, and horrific shrieks from scalded sailors marked the brutality of the escaping steam. Then the air that had been trapped within the ship erupted, vomiting up to the surface a knot of bodies, furniture, spars and yardarms that had all got entangled somewhere within the inverted wreckage.

The *Victoria* continued to spin as she sank, and it was to the creamy pool at the centre of this wheeling circle that a *mélange* of living and dead was inexorably sucked. Many who had not drowned within the vortex were slammed into by the spiralling snarl of metal and wood that had shot up from below; still others were torn to pieces by the screws that continued to run even as the hull, which by this time had turned vertical, plummeted straight down. In less than a quarter of an hour, she was gone.

Caught up in the frenzy of sinking, the *Victoria* had failed to release her lifeboats. Later I would discover that the hydraulics needed to free them no longer operated. Fortunately, the teams of men in the small boats sent out by the other ships were able to retrieve both the living and the dead who floated past in the blood-red sea.

*****

It was just then that I saw some movement among the flotsam floating in my direction—a white-shirted sailor clinging to a spar was washing towards the shore. Once he saw me, he struggled to raise an arm.

Needless to say, I dashed into the small waves and, half-running, half-swimming, grabbed the wood to which he clung and guided it and him to safety. He sputtered his thanks as I helped him stagger from the water. Then I gently lowered him to the sand, where bloodied, worn out, and drenched, he lay panting before me.

"My God," he said at last. And then he repeated it over and over again. "My God. My God."

It took a few minutes for him to catch his breath; but once he settled down, he looked seaward at the limping *Camperdown*, the ship that had crashed into his own. By this time, she had backed well enough away from the point of impact that she seemed ready to drop anchor.

"Are you all right?" I asked. "You've suffered quite a shock."

He looked surprised at my words. I imagine that my Arab garb, along with my sun-baked complexion and bearded face, may have put him off. Hearing me use the Queen's English, however, seemed to assure him that I was a fellow countryman.

He took a few more breaths; and when he appeared to have collected himself, he said, "I'm a midshipman from the *Victoria*, sir. I saw it all."

Had the young man still been wearing his blue frock coat, I would have recognised his relative rank. Wisely, he had taken to the water without it. He'd discarded his shoes as well.

"How came this tragedy?" I asked, "I mean, besides the obvious. How came these two ships to collide?"

The midshipman shook his head. "Stupid," he muttered.

"Sorry?" I pressed him again.

"Admiral Tryon," he gasped.

"Sir George?" Even then I knew the name—Vice-Admiral Sir George Tryon, K.C.B, a big bear of a man with a personality to match—one of the most loved and feared officers in the Royal Navy. A disciple of Lord Nelson, he seldom made mistakes—some would have said, "never".

"Right," said the midshipman, "Sir George."

"What was he thinking?"

The sailor shook his head. "We'd been in Beirut for five days, and we weighed anchor this morning at 9.45. Beirut's forty miles to the south, and it was supposed to take us six-and-a-half hours to get here. We were sailing along quite well at about nine knots. Because of her long, low forecastle, the *Victoria* moves—moved—easily in the water. She was nicknamed "the slipper", you know, because her ride was so smooth. We arrived here right on schedule; and after dividing into two divisions, we headed for the eastern shore."

The midshipman raised a limp forefinger in the direction of the nearby stone ruins. "The Tower of Lions over there," said he. "That was our landmark. The Admiral intended to have the lead ships of both lines turn inward when they reached the head of their columns at a point parallel to the Tower of Lions. That was the plan at any rate. Then we could put in at our anchorage in the same order in which we'd entered the bay."

The young man rubbed a hand across his eyes. As his hair dried in the sun, I could see that it was dark-blond rather than the black it had appeared when I'd fished him out of the water. No doubt he would make quite the smart officer when he advanced.

"Once the Admiral gave the initial order," the midshipman went on, "I saw the other officers exchange looks. To a man, I don't believe any of them thought there was enough distance between the two columns to complete the manoeuvre. The *Victoria* needed at least four cables length to turn."

"Cables?"

"Sorry," he muttered. "About two hundred yards. The *Camperdown* would have required the same. And yet we appeared to be but six cables apart. We probably needed twice that space."

"Did no one question the order?"

The sailor managed a faint smile. "One doesn't question the Commander-in-Chief of the Fleet. Certainly not a midshipman like me. One *should*, of course, if the safety of the ship is threatened. A couple of officers mumbled some concern, but not with any purpose. Still, the danger seemed obvious. I'm convinced that's why Admiral Markham, the commander of the *Camperdown*, was reluctant to begin his own turn."

"'Reluctant', you say?"

"Aye, sir. He failed to respond to Admiral Tryon's initial signal to turn. He hoisted his flag in agreement only after repeated demands were flashed to him from the *Victoria*, and by then we were too close to the shore. There was no time left for either ship; that's when we turned into one another.

"The collision was bad enough—though even then we might have weathered it except for the *Camperdown's* bloody ram—begging your pardon. It holed us below the waterline. When the *Camperdown* backed away, you see, the water rushed into the breach. If the two ships had remained locked together, maybe the *Victoria* wouldn't have sunk. Who's to say? There might have been just enough time to seal the watertight doors and save the ship.

"As it was, we slammed a few doors closed—and, God forgive us, locked in some poor souls by accident. We tried to shut all the doors; but, my God, there was just too much water. The Admiral was trying to reach land; but the distance was more than four miles, and we couldn't move any faster than four knots. Then there were the heavy guns near the prow. They weighed her down. Once she tipped forward—well, in seventy fathoms of water the result was inevitable."

"Did Admiral Tryon say nothing?"

"As we were going down, I heard him talking to another officer. 'My fault,' the Admiral said. 'It is entirely my doing, entirely my fault.' And then he was gone. I myself was thrown free. Thank God, I grabbed onto something that floated by. I managed to tear off my coat and shoes and hold on till you came to my aid."

Clearly exhausted, the poor fellow leaned back. Talking to me had worn him out. Meanwhile, the rescue missions continued. Small boat after small boat returned to land filled with the quick and the dead.

Suddenly, we were engulfed in a shadow. A figure from out of nowhere loomed over us and eclipsed the sun. It was a naval officer, who had seen the two of us conversing. With his black-billed white hat and dark-blue frock coat in perfect order, he commanded the midshipman to stand and report to the docks where inventories of the survivors were being completed.

"Under no circumstances," the officer commanded as the bedraggled sailor shakily got to his feet, "are you to speak with anyone about what occurred here this afternoon. Do you understand?"

"Aye, sir," said the midshipman.

The young man and I exchanged glances. I trust he realised that the Royal Navy would hear nothing from me about what he had said. With a trembling hand, he saluted his superior, completed a ragged about turn, and marched off as best he could. I had not even learned his name.

The officer now looked *me* over from head to toe. Thanks to my local dress, I suspect he saw no cause for worry. Whom was *I* going to tell? Besides, the collision—a deadly accident of the greatest magnitude—had been a naval flummox of the grandest order; and though I knew the Royal Navy to be reluctant to announce its failings, I could not imagine that the Admiralty would consider attempting to conceal so horrific a mistake.

I was wrong, of course; but it took a night in a small hotel and plenty of thought to make me reconsider my silence. Upon Friday, having decided to report the disaster I had witnessed, I returned to the same telegraph office from where I had cabled you, Mycroft. Although I hoped my look of assurance the day before had conveyed to the midshipman that I would not report to the Navy what he had told me, I had not intended such an understanding to prohibit my communicating with Fleet Street. The public deserved to know what had occurred that fateful summer's day.

*****

The same diminutive clerk was sitting at the same barren desk he had been facing the day before. It was as if he had not moved. Perhaps if I spoke distinctly enough, he would understand me. "I need to cable London," said I slowly. "About the collision at sea."

"You're wasting your time," said a gentleman with an American accent. "The news is already abroad."

In so great a hurry when I had entered the office, I failed to notice the man standing to the right of the door. He had been leaning both elbows on the counter, and now he removed his straw hat to mop his bald head with a well-used handkerchief. Perspiring freely, he wore neither collar nor necktie; and dressed in wilted white shirt and trousers, he looked overwhelmed by the heat. He seemed to perk up, however, when he heard me informing the telegraph operator that I intended to send a wire about the naval tragedy.

"I appreciate that you want to tell the world what happened here yesterday, but that fellow"— he gestured with his straw hat towards the clerk, "doesn't speak any English. Besides, like I said, the world already knows."

"I can well imagine," said I.

Though I felt thwarted in my personal plans, news that the story had got out made perfect sense to me. At the time, I did not know of Rear-Admiral Markham's cable to the Sea Lords describing the collision, but I none the less assumed that some official would be duty-bound to send the Admiralty a report.

"And yet they want more," said the man, raising a forefinger portentously.

"Who?"

"The press, who else? Pierre, the cable operator over there, showed me a request that's just come in from London. Since he doesn't read the language, he asked me for help. I'm Ira Harris, by the way," said he, extending his hand, "Dr Ira Harris from Fayetteville, New York."

I clasped his hand, responding with my Sigerson alias.

"Glad to meet you," said he. "For a Norwegian, you're pretty far from base. I'm with the Presbyterian Board

144

of Foreign Missions—been running the Tripoli Hospital here for the past ten years. The locals trust me."

"What did you mean," I asked, "when you said 'they want more'?"

The American slid a wrinkled, yellow cablegram along the counter-top to me. It had been lying in front of him, but was actually addressed "To the Telegraph Agent, Tripoli, Syria". The printed message had come from an American pressman in London called David Graham Phillips of the *World*. To my astonishment, he was offering $500 for two thousand words about the naval disaster, which he had somehow got wind of.

"Any such offers from the *British* press?" I asked. *"The Times? The Evening Standard? The Daily News?"*

"No," Dr Harris answered, shaking his head, "not one. But I can vouch for the *World*. I've been a subscriber for years."

"Well then," said I, clapping my hands together, "I see no good reason to deprive this Mr Graham Phillips of the story—if we can figure out a way to send it, that is. At least, he's in London."

"Tell me what you know," Harris offered, reaching for a pencil and blank sheet of paper on a nearby table. "I'll write it down in big block letters so that Pierre here can read it. Without knowing any English, he can still copy the words and send them off."

Having got Pierre to dispatch my own cable to Mycroft the day before, I understood the procedure and agreed to the doctor's proposition. Careful not to identify my source, I combined the first-hand experience that the midshipman had described to me with what I myself had observed. Taken together, the two accounts produced a comprehensive narrative of the terrible collision.

Dr Harris took it all down slowly whilst I kept an eye out the window. I remained on the lookout for suspicious naval authorities seeking to quash any news that might be heading for England. Since I had already been scrutinised once by such a figure, I decided to exit the office as soon as I had finished my report, trusting the American to see that the message would be safely sent.

It was years later that I came to learn how much responsibility I had placed on the poor man. It took Dr Harris and Pierre until 10.00 that night to compose the piece; and only then did the doctor discover that in order to send so lengthy a story to London, it first had to be relayed from Tripoli's central office to Beirut. Not only did it require another hour for Dr Harris to reach the central office by tram and foot; but upon reaching the place, he had to wait an additional thirty minutes for the operator, who also knew no English, to finish his cigar. Once again, Dr Harris was required to spell out each word of the story. What's more— much to his credit in light of what he had already experienced—he borrowed $500 from an acquaintance to facilitate the money exchange that Graham Phillips had originally promised to Pierre.

I suppose one could say that the rest is history. In spite of the pressures that the Admiralty put on Fleet Street to hush up an account of the British Navy's incompetence, Pulitzer's *New York World* could publish the news with impunity. As Watson can attest, after my own role in securing the details was made public a couple of years later, Graham Phillips himself came round Baker Street to thank me.

Actually, I have always believed that Phillips did quite a nice job with the story. Who can forget his terrifying description of the screws? "Frightful, swift, revolving knives," he called them. It was indeed a horror, but a horror that cried out for reporting—and not only for the sheer drama of the event. One could but hope that the news of so catastrophic an accident would provide the impetus for strengthening our military. It was a decade ago that this horrific accident occurred, gentlemen; but even then the winds of war were blowing. Preparation is all, and the collision at sea needed to be exposed as a warning. How else to know of our ironclads' vulnerability? How else to encourage officers to question perilous orders? Indeed, how else, gentlemen, to hold the Royal Navy accountable?

III

Sherlock Holmes refilled his copita and drank more port.

Throughout his brother's narrative, Mycroft had sat fidgeting with his watch chain, constantly checking the time, as if he could scarcely wait for the misguided tale to conclude. Save for the light cast by the electric street lamps outside, the world beyond the bow window had turned black.

"Quite important for you, was it, Sherlock," asked Mycroft at last, "to tell an American pressman all about our mishap—all about one of the greatest peacetime naval disasters in the history of the world? Content to wash our soiled linen in public, were you?"

My friend offered a slight smile. "I believe I told Watson during that business with the busts of Napoleon that the press is a most valuable institution if one only knows how to use it."

I did not recall the quotation, but made a note to employ it if I ever recorded that singular case. Or perhaps I would insert it in another.

"Well, brother-mine," grunted Mycroft Holmes as with no little effort he leaned forward refill his glass, "I should imagine that now it falls upon me *to set the record straight—as much as one can, anyhow." He sighed and fortified himself with another pull.*

For his part, Sherlock Holmes drew a Havana from an inner pocket, struck a Vespa, and lit the cigar. In anticipation of his brother's speech, Holmes leaned back into his chair and stretched out his long legs. Almost immediately, the cloying smell of his tobacco filled the room.

IV

Mycroft Holmes's Account

We came here tonight, gentlemen, to mourn the dead. And yet as I might have predicted, our memorial has unfortunately devolved into yet another recapitulation of the tragic events that occurred this day ten years ago. How many times must one hear the agonizing details? No doubt, the fault is mine for suggesting this remembrance in the first place—unless, of course, this new vexation is simply the price one pays for having failed to reveal all the facts ten years ago. There is, you see, more to the story of the collision than both of you are aware—much of which, I'm pleased to say, the Foreign Office has now permitted me to share with you.

To begin with, the true subject of this discussion should not be some broad question regarding the military readiness of our forces at sea. Not that such issues are not relevant, mind, but in discussing the tragedy of *H.M.S. Victoria*, the focus must really centre upon a single plot—the attempt by the Germans to steal an object that *was*—and in all probability still *is*—the greatest artefact in the possession of the Royal Navy—certainly, in the possession of the Mediterranean Fleet. I am referring to no less than the grand battle sword of Vice-Admiral Horatio Lord Nelson, the same sword that Nelson brandished in his epic victory over Napoleon—in a word, gentlemen, the very quintessence of British naval supremacy. I need not overstate how the loss of such a treasure would convulse the nation.

Yet in addition to so keen a symbol of British military might, there was in the early nineties an even greater matter concerning the country. Oh, I freely acknowledge that you didn't know it at the time, Sherlock; but when the dispatch that you composed concerning the naval accident in Tripoli was sent off to David Graham Phillips, you were in effect tinkering with the political equilibrium of all Europe. Truth to tell, gentlemen, we meet here this very night during a grave period of contemporary history. Current diplomatic efforts bear significant implications for the fate of the entire world, a fate that the ten-year-old collision of the *Camperdown* and the *Victoria* may actually have played some role in shaping.

You will recall that it was just a few weeks ago that His Majesty King Edward travelled to Paris, and it is now but a few weeks prior to the reciprocal trip to these islands of French President Loubet. As I'm sure you are both aware, the purpose of these meetings is highly political—to finalise the agreement called the *Entente Cordiale*, an understanding between France and England that will solidify the bonds between our two nations in the face of growing German strength—growing German strength at *sea* in particular.

As you know, under the guise of an intricate balance of power, the late German Chancellor, Otto Von Bismarck, worked hard at masking his goal of German hegemony. As a consequence, for more than a decade now, England and France have been striving to confound the Kaiser's ambitious wiles and weaken the strength of the German Empire. Not with much success, I am afraid. With French and British concerns on the one hand and the Kaiser's subversive schemes on the other, I fear this competition can have but one result. Personally, I cannot envision another decade slipping past without a monstrous confrontation among the nations of Europe.

But enough about the future, gentlemen. Let us not forget that we are here tonight to memorialise the past. Which brings us back to that terrible day in June of 1893. Allow me to set the stage. Recall that in the early nineties the Royal Navy was *nonpareil*. The Germans hoped to match us, but simply could not. And yet, ironically, it was the very *lack* of opposition, which was based on our strengths, that engendered complacency in our ranks.

Sir George Tryon rightly believed that, short of having an enemy at whom to fire, confronting our navy with challenging manoeuvres remained our next-best chance of staying alert. As Commander-in-Chief of the Mediterranean Fleet, Sir George put his ships through their paces, as it were, inspiring them to conduct all sorts of innovative drills and in the process display the Union Jack to all the sheiks and sultans of the area—not to mention any potentates of Europe—who might be observing the manoeuvres.

As for his vessel, as you rightly noted, Sherlock, *H.M.S. Victoria* was the flagship of the Fleet. The Admiralty was most proud of her. Her 100,000 tons of steel made her among the largest, fastest, most powerful ironclads in the world. With two 16.25-inch, 111-ton guns, the largest in the Royal Navy, she was also the best protected. Why, within the Mediterranean Fleet alone, we possessed six of the most feared battleships afloat.

All of which made the sinking of the *Victoria* so distressing. The Sea Lords received word of the tragedy at 12.30 the morning after—twenty-two officers killed; over three hundred men lost. That a first-class warship costing close to one-million pounds could capsize in ten minutes and completely sink in thirteen called into question the fundamental designs of our most important ships.

Take the *Victoria's* side-armour, for example. It stopped short of encasing the entire hull. Would extending it further have protected her from the *Camperdown's* ram? And what of her heavy guns? Would not lesser weapons have increased the time it took her to sink? For that matter, what about the chain of command throughout the Navy? As you suggested earlier, Sherlock, should we have been doing more to encourage officers to countermand orders that seemed to threaten the safety of the ship? The Admiralty wanted answers. After all, if such a catastrophe was the result of a mere collision, what damage could enemy guns produce?

We can surely agree that resolving such difficulties is vital to military success, and yet in point of fact these questions bear little relation to what was actually going on that day ten years ago. What you did not know then, Sherlock—and what the Foreign Office is allowing me to tell you tonight—concerns a German plot set into motion during the early summer ten years ago when a small band of English-speaking German spies arrived somewhere on the coast of Syria and, disguised as British bluejackets, eventually managed to insert themselves among the *Victoria's* crew.

You already mentioned, Sherlock, that it was no secret how much Vice-Admiral Tryon admired Lord Nelson. Indeed, an avid collector of all matters related to his beloved hero, Sir George had made large purchases at an auction featuring many of Nelson's valuables. The prize of the collection was the famous battle sword that we have previously discussed—the same sword, incidentally, which served as model for the blade held by Nelson's statue atop the Corinthian column in Trafalgar Square. (Do you know that in the daylight one can almost see it from this very window?) And, of course, it was public knowledge that the artefact in question was hanging on display in Sir George's cabin aboard the *Victoria*.

Because of the sword's great symbolic value, the German high command—perhaps, von Tirpitz himself, their *Kapitän zur See*—were bent on stealing the thing. In fact, once the Kaiser heard about it, he himself became obsessed with obtaining the blade. You can understand their nefarious thinking. What better way for the German Imperial Navy to demonstrate its dominance over the greatest naval force in the world than by securing so valuable a possession?

It was the job of those German spies who had been set down in Syria to masquerade as English sailors and grab the sword. They planned to steal it as the *Victoria* was sailing into port at Tripoli and then commandeer the ship away from the fleet and escape via a commercial vessel waiting for them at the docks. Even though it was staring you in the face, Sherlock, I doubt that you noticed the merchant ship flying the German flag that day. She had been anchored in the harbour to be used in their getaway.

No? I thought not.

How many Germans there were and how and where they masterfully infiltrated themselves among the hundreds of sailors aboard the *Victoria*—not to mention how the Admiralty got wind of the plan—all this I am not at liberty to reveal. Actually, no one with whom I have ever discussed the matter understands just how much of the scheme the Sea Lords knew. I was told that the Admiralty had hoped to send a secret group of marines to overtake the Germans in Beirut, but that our men could not be deployed quickly enough.

The remainder of this story, I'm afraid, is all rather hearsay. There were rumours to the effect that Vice-Admiral Tryon knew about the secret contingent of marines aboard the *Camperdown* and that he formulated a scheme to enable the marines to board the *Victoria* when the two ships met. Bringing the ships close enough for such a transfer may be the reason that, even with such insufficient space between the two, he so ill advisedly attempted the evolution. Sir George, dynamic officer that he was, apparently had no fear of executing the manoeuvre. The German merchant ship left port just moments after the disastrous collision. As for the spies stranded on the *Victoria,* one supposes that those who were not killed in the accident somehow managed to escape. Whatever their fate, they were officially listed as "presumed dead".

Unfortunately, Sherlock, you were present to witness the results of a plan gone awry. As you have already described, within minutes of having been penetrated by the *Camperdown's* ram, the *Victoria* plummeted prow first straight down to the bottom of the Mediterranean. Our mathematical experts conjecture that it must have stuck upright like an arrow shot into the ground. They surmise that it hit with such force that some three-quarters of the hull buried itself into the ocean's floor. It goes without saying, of course, that even now, a decade later, the sword of Lord Nelson remains somewhere within the wreckage.

*****

Enter the American, Mr David Graham Phillips.

Following the receipt of Rear-Admiral Markham's dispatch that arrived after midnight in London, the Admiralty assumed that some news of the affair was bound to leak out to the public. According to the Foreign Office, however, Phillips had access to more official sources than do most pressmen. It seems that he maintained contact with a Portuguese minister who in turn had informants in the Turkish Embassy. It was through these channels that news of a major disaster in the Mediterranean was first reported.

Much to the dismay of the Ministry of Defence, the British press did manage to print a few lines about the affair but nothing of any significance. And yet this mere whiff of trouble was sufficient to inspire the publicity-seeking Phillips to gamble two shillings per word for any additional news regarding the accident. As you know, Sherlock, it was upon Friday, the day after the collision, that Phillips sent the cablegram to Tripoli offering money for the story to the telegraph agent, the man you identified as Pierre.

Though Phillips received Pierre's answer on Saturday evening—"Will send account," it read—by early Monday morning Phillips had yet to receive any details. Nor, for that matter, had any British newspapers. But then, at 11.00, half a dozen sentences about the collision began trickling into the *World's* London office; minutes later, some more came in, and every ten minutes thereafter another batch arrived until the report was completed. These cables, of course, comprised the account that you gave to Dr Harris, Sherlock, which he, thanks to the Herculean effort you have already described, managed to have telegraphed to London.

For his part, Phillips made these facts known throughout the world. I'll give the man his due. He pulled no punches when it came to laying blame. He called Vice-Admiral Tryon an "insane commander" and the decision to turn the ship inward an "insane order". He compared the sinking of the *Victoria* to the "sounding" of a whale.

And yet, in retrospect, I suppose it was fortunate for the American that Mr Pulitzer denied him a by-line. That way, you see, Phillips himself was able to dodge much of the anger the Admiralty aimed at those papers deemed to have revealed too much about what had occurred in the Mediterranean that fateful day.

On the other hand, to deflect any criticism regarding Fleet Street's inability to acquire the relevant facts, British publishers labelled the *World's* story a "fake". Presumptuous, to be sure—and ironical as well. For not only did the attack by the British papers fail, but in the end most of them felt duty-bond to reprint in full the *World's* initial report.

As I am sure you have already inferred, gentlemen, it was political motivation that caused the Admiralty to quash any news of the collision. First and foremost, they worried that if Germany's secret role in the ugly affair had become known, the war hawks in Whitehall would have demanded a military response—a response, which, thanks to the Kaiser's newly built navy, we could not be confident of winning. It also did not help to advertise how easily the Germans had infiltrated our forces. Fortunately, at least that part of the story has never reached the public.

But there was still more about the accident that needed to be contained. With German sea power growing, the Sea Lords wanted to suppress any news concerning the vulnerability of our sturdiest warships. Iron clad, heavily armed, strongly powered—it all mattered not a whit if the things could sink to the bottom of the sea within thirteen minutes!

And that was not the worst of the affair. One cannot forget the humiliation—the loss of more than three-hundred able-bodied seamen due to the miscalculation of an overly aggressive commander! At so delicate a time, we could not afford trumpeting to the world the news of what was perhaps the greatest blunder in the history of the Royal Navy. And all for the desire of an antique sword!

So at long last, brother, we come to the crux of our disagreement. *You* believe people have the right to know what happened; *I* believe that in light of the welfare of the country, the government has the right to control such information. I willingly acknowledge that your position is the more noble. Mine, however, is the more practical; for my position ultimately allows philosophers like you to breathe the air that enables them to speak of freedom.

I have talked quite enough now. It is time for more liquid refreshment.

V

Mycroft drank rapidly his glass of port and then turned to stare at his brother.

Staring right back, Sherlock Holmes exhaled a cloud of smoke. He seemed to be searching for an appropriate response as he slowly laid his cigar in a nearby ashtray. It was none too soon; for by now, a tenebrous haze had filled most of the room.

"Are you aware, Mycroft," he drawled at last, *"that in his* Areopagitica*, the great Englishman John Milton wrote the following:* 'Give me the liberty to know, to utter, and to argue freely according to conscience, above all liberties'?*"*

Waving away the smoke, Mycroft Holmes offered the same slight smile that I had seen on many an occasion in the muted reactions of his brother.

"And are you aware, Sherlock," said Mycroft drily, *"that in his great monument to British freedom called 'On Liberty', John Stuart Mill wrote:* 'Despotism is a legitimate mode of government in dealing with barbarians'?*"*

Nostrils flaring, Sherlock Holmes sat up straight as he prepared his riposte. *"Speaking of your new friends, the French,"* he hissed, steel-grey eyes flashing with menace, *"no less a figure than Voltaire has said*: 'Je déteste ce que vous écrivez, mais je donnerai ma vie pour que vous puissiez continuer à écrire.'*"*

"Hah!" Mycroft exclaimed. *"'Niemand ist mehr Sklave, als der sich für frei hält, ohne es zu sein'.* *As if a punctuation mark were needed, he spat out the single name* "Goethe".

I understood the French. In point of fact, while the sentiment *about writing free from censorship was most assuredly Voltaire's, there was some lingering controversy about whether the words themselves—"I detest what you write, but I will give my life so that you may continue to write"—were actually those of the Frenchman.*

As for the German, I looked to Mycroft for a translation; but Sherlock Holmes answered me first: *"'None are more hopelessly enslaved than those who falsely believe they are free'."*

Mycroft seethed at having been outdone by his gloating brother. Grotesque mirror images, both men sat warily eyeing the other, each breathing heavily, as if he had just completed a mile-long foot race. For my part, I might as well have not even been there.

It was Mycroft who finally broke the uncomfortable silence. "We must do nothing to endanger the fragile Franco-British alliance that is being constructed as we speak. Mark my words, brother-mine—war is in the offing. We can ill afford to fight among ourselves when we should be working together to build solid resolve."

Sherlock Holmes raised his glass of port. "Agreed," said he. "But don't forget that we also agreed to let friend Watson here decide which one of us has proffered the more compelling argument."

To be honest, I was hoping that they had indeed forgotten the proposition. But Mycroft touched his glass to his brother's, and they sipped their port. Holmes picked up his Havana, and then both combatants turned to me.

"Well, Watson," said my friend, "what do you make of it all?"

Now I have been in tight fixes before, and I have never lost my nerve—not whilst facing Jezail bullets in Afghanistan nor stalking that supernatural hound in the Grimpen Mire nor even being shot just a year before by "Killer" Evans. And yet all those dire predicaments paled when compared to fending off the imperial gaze of the brothers Holmes for a second time in a single evening. Like gimlets, their sharp eyes bore into m; and I feared alienating either one.

I needed to gain additional time for consideration of my answer. Opening a window would serve the purpose.

"Fresh air," I explained as I rose from my chair.

"Do you not find," asked Mycroft, "that a concentrated atmosphere enables one to maintain more concentrated thoughts?"

"There is a limit," said I definitively—though Mycroft's remark had a familiar ring. I seemed to recall hearing something similar from his brother early in our investigation of the Baskerville business. Perhaps the observation was a family tenet. I let it go, however, and raised the sash, content to inhale the cool night air.

At the same time, I considered my alternatives. In point of fact, the arguments of both brothers warranted defending. As a writer, I could easily support what America's Bill of Rights calls "the freedom of the press". No author on earth wants to be censored. And yet, whilst the sanctity of the written word demands preservation, the siren song of military preparedness also clamours to be heard. In my heart, I could feel the correctness of the writer's calling; in my brain, I could not ignore the voice of reason. I needed to establish a middle ground.

It was whilst returning to my chair that I experienced the epiphany. Suddenly, I recognised the goal of both of the brothers. Ignore their lofty language, I thought. It was with the author of a theory—not with the theory itself—that each brother really wanted me to side. Of course. Once I determined that this standoff was more personal than philosophical, my role became clear. More important than deciding which principle to support was encouraging each brother to make peace with the other.

Thus it was that I settled on the word "compromise" as a solution to my dilemma. It would be the tool that would guide me between this modern Scylla and Charybdis. "Compromise" may seem a simple remedy, for it is a course of action tolerated and even respected by most people in a civilised society. But then the two men sitting before me did not represent "most people"; and to judge by my own experiences, I expected neither one to appreciate my conclusion. And yet, in truth, I regarded my attempts to reconcile the pair to be among the most challenging situations I had ever faced.

"Gentlemen," said I, waving my hand to clear the air, "this is nothing but a silly feud between two siblings. Forget the fate of the Victoria and Nelson's sword. That business took place ten years ago. As of now, one can only assume that each of you has solidified the righteousness of your own position in order to trivialise that of your brother. Simply put, Mr Sherlock Holmes, you must recognise that, like many a criminal investigation, matters of state require caution when one makes them public. Mr Mycroft Holmes, for your part, you must accept that, like many a political moment, the public require the Truth and will somehow—and sometimes at great cost—work hard to discover it."

During the silence that ensued, it was obvious to me that both men recognised the fundamental principles I was exhorting. Yet I must point out that whenever brothers are involved, not even the skills of a master arbitrator can be counted upon to settle disputes. Cain's treatment of Abel aptly dramatizes the situation.

To my great relief, however, simultaneous sighs finally broke the stillness. The penetrating gazes that had fallen upon me now turned to focus more softly on each other. The two men spoke at the same time.

"Quite right," said my friend.

"Just so," said Mycroft.

And the two brothers leaned toward each other and clasped hands.

"You know, you're quite correct, Watson," said Sherlock Holmes, "and yet even as you artfully unite the two of us, I fear that all of Europe will soon be in need of statesmen like yourself. For who else will be capable of resolving the hostility that Mycroft so rightly describes as permeating the atmosphere?

"No matter our resolutions here tonight, the world remains divided; and ultimately all of us will have to take a stand. For battle-lines will be drawn, old fellow, and I fear that even the greatest of nations will be unable to field ministers with your admirable negotiating skills. Soon we shall all be forced to choose. What then*? Must we muzzle the voices of liberty in the name of our security?"*

"Whatever we do, Sherlock," Mycroft answered, "friend Watson here is quite right. We must do it together."

It was not often that I intervened in the life of my friend and colleague Mr Sherlock Holmes. Seldom was I given the opportunity. But as we all shared a final drink together that evening, I knew that I for one should always regard my reconciliation of the two Holmes brothers as one of the bravest and most noble deeds I have ever done. *

* More information about the naval disaster may be found in Richard Hough's *Admirals in Collision* and in "A Famous Newspaper Beat," the chapter in Isaac F. Marcosson's *David Graham Phillips and His Times* that deals exclusively with Phillips's reporting of the story. (DDV)

One final point: *HMS Victoria* still remains buried where she sank in 1893, some 500 feet below the surface of the Mediterranean Sea off the coast of what is now Lebanon. In early 2012, however, news media reported that eight years earlier an explorer and salvage-diver named Mark Ellyatt had actually discovered Lord Nelson's treasured sword within the wreckage. To avoid issues over ownership, the Ministry of Defence requested that the coveted artefact be left on board the *Victoria*, and Ellyatt complied, admitting that he had hidden the sword somewhere within the ruins of the submerged ship. *The Daily Mail* has suggested that for the sword alone collectors would pay up to one million pounds.